*A
Harlequin
Romance*

OTHER
Harlequin Romances
by BETTY NEELS

Many of these titles are available at your local bookseller,
or through the Harlequin Reader Service.

For a free catalogue listing all available Harlequin Romances,
send your name and address to:

HARLEQUIN READER SERVICE,
M.P.O. Box 707, Niagara Falls, N.Y. 14302
Canadian address: Stratford, Ontario, Canada.

or use order coupon at back of book.

STARS THROUGH THE MIST

by

BETTY NEELS

HARLEQUIN BOOKS   TORONTO
WINNIPEG

Original hard cover edition published in 1973
by Mills & Boon Limited.

© Betty Neels 1973

SBN 373-01761-8

Harlequin edition published March 1974

Printed in Canada

1761

CHAPTER ONE

THE operating theatre was a hive of industry, its usual hush giving way to sudden utterances of annoyance or impatience as the nurses went briskly to and fro about their business. Sister Deborah Culpeper, arranging her instruments with efficient speed on the trolley before her, found time to listen to the plaintive wail of her most junior nurse, who was unable to find the Langenbeck retractors she had been sent to fetch, while at the same time keeping an eye on Bob, the theatre technician, who was trying out the electrical equipment needed for the various drills which would presently be needed. She calmed the nurse, nodded approval of Bob's efforts, begged Staff Nurse Perkins to get the dressings laid out in their correct order and glanced at the clock.

One minute to nine o'clock, and as far as she could see, everything was ready. She swung the trolley round with an expert kick and then stood, relaxed and calm, behind it, knowing that in a few minutes the rest of the staff would follow suit; she never badgered them or urged them on, merely saw to it that each nurse had her fair share of the work and time enough in which to do it. She looked ahead of her now, apparently at the tiled wall opposite her, aware of every last move being made, nothing of her visible beneath the green gown which enveloped her, only her dark eyes showing above the mask. She looked the picture of calm self-assurance, and her nurses, aware of their own hurried breath and rapid pulses, envied her. A quite unwarranted feeling, as it happened, for despite her outward tranquillity, Deborah's heart had quickened its pace to an alarming rate, and her breath, despite her efforts to keep it firmly under her control, had run mad. She gave her head a tiny, vexed shake, for it annoyed her very much that she should behave so stupidly whenever Mr van Doorninck was operating; she had tried every means in her power to remain uncaring of his presence and had mastered her feelings so well that she could present a placid front to him when they met and subdue those same feelings so sternly that she could scarcely be faulted as a perfect Theatre Sister; only on his operating days did her feelings get a little out of hand, something which she thanked heaven she could conceal behind her mask. She looked up now as the patient was wheeled in, arranged with nicety upon the operating table and covered with a blanket, to be followed immediately by the opening of the swing doors at the further end of the theatre and the appearance of two men.

Deborah's lovely eyes swept over the shorter, younger man—the Registrar, Peter Jackson—and rested briefly upon Mr van Doorninck. He was a very tall man with broad shoulders shrouded, as was every one else, in green theatre garb. His eyes above the mask swept round the theatre now, missing nothing as he walked to the table. His good morning to Sister Culpeper was affable if somewhat reserved, and his glance from under heavy lids was brief. She returned his greeting in a quiet, detached voice and turned at once to her trolley, wondering for the hundredth time how it was possible for a sensible woman of twenty-seven to be so hopelessly and foolishly in love with a consultant

6

surgeon who had never uttered more than a few brief conventional phrases to her. But in love she was, and during the two years in which she had worked for him, it had strengthened into a depth of feeling which had caused her to refuse two proposals of marriage. She sighed soundlessly and began the familiar ritual of arranging the sterile sheets and towels over the unconscious form on the table.

She worked with speed and care, knowing exactly how the silent man on the other side of the table liked them arranged; in two years she had got to know quite a lot about him—that he was even-tempered but never easy-going, that when the occasion warranted it, he could display a cold anger, that he was kind and considerate and reticent about himself—almost taciturn. But of his life outside the theatre she knew very little; he was yearned over by the student nurses to whom he gave lectures, sought after by the more senior female staff, and openly laid siege to by the prettier, younger nurses. No one knew where he lived or what he did with his spare time; from time to time he let drop the information that he was either going to Holland or had just returned. The one fact which emerged from the wealth of rumour which surrounded him was that he was not married—an interesting detail which had increased the efforts of the young women who rather fancied themselves as his wife. And once or twice he had mentioned to Deborah that he had parents in Holland, as well as brothers and a sister who had been to England to visit him. Deborah had longed to ask questions and had restrained herself, knowing that if she did he would probably never tell her anything again.

She finished the preliminaries, glanced at him, and at his 'Ready, Sister?' gave her usual placid 'Yes, sir,' and handed him the towel clips which he liked to arrange for himself. After that she kept her thoughts strictly upon her job—scalpel, artery forceps, retractors, and then as he reached the bone, the lion forceps, the Langenbeck retractors, the rugines, the bone levers—she handed each in turn a second or so before he put out his hand to receive them, admiring, as she always did, his smooth technique and the sureness of his work. Not for nothing had he won a place on the top rung of the orthopaedic surgeon's ladder.

The patient was a young man with a malignant tumour of the femur; his only chance of recovery was extensive excision, a proceeding which Mr van Doorninck was undertaking now. Beyond a muttered word now and then to his registrar or a request for some special instrument, he spoke little; only when the operation was three parts completed and they were stitching up did he remark: 'There's a good chance of complete recovery here— as soon as he's fit we'll get him fitted with a leg— remind me to talk to Sister Prosser about him, Peter.'

He turned away from the table and took off his gloves to fling them into one of the bowls and walked out of the theatre, back into the scrubbing-up room, leaving Peter to supervise the removal of the patient and Deborah to organise the preparation of the theatre for the next case, reflecting as she did so that Sister Prosser, plain and plump and fifty if she was a day, was the most envied member of the nursing staff, because she saw Mr van Doorninck every day, and not only that, he took coffee with her frequently, and was known to have a great respect for her opinion of his patients' conditions.

The morning wore on; a child next with a Ewing's tumour over which the surgeon frowned and muttered to Peter, knowing that his careful surgery offered little hope of a permanent cure, then an old lady whose broken thigh was to be pinned and plated. It was like a carpenter's shop, thought Deborah, expertly changing drills and listening to the high whine of the electric equipment Bob was obediently switching on and off; what with drills and saws and mallets, it was a noisy way to spend a morning, although after five years of it she should be used to it. She had always been interested in bones and when she had finished her training and had had an opportunity of taking the post of staff nurse in the orthopaedic theatre, she had jumped at the chance, and a year later, when the Theatre Sister had retired, she had taken over her job, content with her lot—there was time enough to think about getting married in a year or two, in the meantime she would make a success of her new post, something she had done in a very short time so that there still seemed no urgency to take the idea of marriage seriously.

She was twenty-five when Mr van Doorninck walked into the theatre unit one day, to be introduced as the new orthopaedic consultant, and from that moment she had felt no desire to marry anyone at all, only him. She had realised how hopeless her wish was within a short time, and being a girl with common sense, had told herself to stop being a fool, and had accepted numerous invitations from a

9

number of the younger doctors in the hospital. She had taken trips in fast sports cars, attended classical concerts, and visited cinemas and theatres, according to her escorts' tastes, but it hadn't helped in the least; she was left with the feeling that she had wasted her time as well as that of all the young men who had taken her out, for Mr van Doorninck's image remained clearly imprinted inside her head and refused to be budged.

She had come to realise over the last few months that there was only one way of escape from his unconscious toils; she would have to leave Clare's and start all over again somewhere else. Indeed she had already put this plan into effect, searching the *Nursing Times* for a suitable post, preferably situated at the furthest possible point from London.

They had a break for coffee after the old lady's fragile bones had been reinforced by Mr van Doorninck's expert carpentry. The talk was of the patients, naturally enough, but with their second cups, the two men began a discussion on the merits of the Registrar's new car and Deborah slipped away to scrub and relieve Staff for her own elevenses. They were still discussing cars when the theatre party reassembled around the table again to tackle a nasty shattered elbow, which Mr van Doorninck patiently fitted together like a jigsaw puzzle with Peter's help, several lengths of wire, a screw or two, and the electric drill again. That done to his satisfaction, he turned his attention to the last case, added hastily to the list at the last minute, because the patient had only been admitted early that morning with a fractured pelvis after he had crashed on his motor bike. It took longer than Deborah had expected. Half way through the operation she signed to Staff and one of the nurses to go to lunch, which left her with Bob and a very junior nurse, who, though willing and eager to please, was inclined to blunder around. It was long past two o'clock when the case left the theatre, and Mr van Doorninck, with a politely worded apology for running so far over his usual time, went too. She wouldn't see him again until Thursday; he operated three times a week and today was Monday.

The afternoon was spent doing the washdown in the theatre, and Deborah, on duty until Staff should relieve her at five o'clock, retired to her office to attend to the paper work. She had discarded her theatre gown and mask and donned her muslin cap in order to go to the dining room for her late dinner; now she spent a few moments repairing the ravages of a busy morning—not that they showed overmuch; her very slightly tiptilted nose shone just a little, her hair, which she wore drawn back above a wide forehead, still retained the smooth wings above each cheek and the heavy coil in her neck was still firmly skewered. She applied lipstick to her large, well-shaped mouth, passed a wetted fingertip across her dark brows, put her cap back on, and stared at the result.

She had been told times out of number that she was a very pretty girl, indeed, one or two of her more ardent admirers had gone so far as to say that she was beautiful. She herself, while not conceited, found her face passably good-looking but nothing out of the ordinary, but she, of course, was unaware of the delight of her smile, or the way her eyes crinkled so nicely at their corners when she laughed, and those same eyes were unusually dark,

11

the colour of pansies, fringed with long curling lashes which were the envy of her friends. She pulled a face at her reflection and turned her back on it to sit at the desk and apply herself to the miscellany upon it, but after ten minutes or so she laid down her pen and picked up the latest copy of the *Nursing Times*; perhaps there would be a job in it which might suit her.

There was—miles away in Scotland. The hospital was small, it was true, but busy, and they wanted an energetic working Sister, able to organise and teach student nurses the secrets of orthopaedics. She marked it with a cross and went back to her writing, telling herself that it was just exactly what she had been looking for, but as she applied herself once more to the delicate task of giving days off to her staff without disrupting the even flow of work, several doubts crept into her mind; not only was the hospital a satisfying distance from Mr van Doorninck, it was also, unfortunately, an unsatisfying distance from her own home. Holidays, not to mention days off, would be an almost impossible undertaking. She went home to Somerset several times a year now, and once a month, when she had her long weekend, she drove herself down in the Fiat 500 she had bought cheap from one of the housemen. She frowned, trying to remember her geography, wondering if Somerset was further away from the northern coasts of Scotland than was London. She could always spend a night with her Aunt Mary who lived on the edge of a hamlet rejoicing in the incredible name of Twice Brewed, hard by Hadrian's Wall, but even then she would have to spend another night on the road. And what was she going to tell her friends when they found out that she intended to leave? She had no good reason for doing so, she had never been anything but happy until Mr van Doorninck turned up and destroyed her peace of mind, and even now she was happy in a way because she was sure of seeing him three times a week at least. She frowned. Put like that, it sounded ridiculous—she would have to find some really sensible reason for giving in her notice. She picked up her pen once more; she would puzzle it out later, when she was off duty.

But there was no opportunity; she had forgotten that it was Jenny Reed's birthday and that they were all going out together to the cinema, so she spent the rest of the evening with half a dozen of the younger Sisters and shelved her problems.

There wasn't much time to think next day either, for the three victims of a car crash were admitted in the early hours of the morning and she was summoned early to go on duty and open up the theatre. Staff was already there when she arrived and so was the junior nurse, her eyes round with excitement as she began the humbler routine tasks which fell to her lot.

'Oh, Sister,' she breathed, 'they're in an awful bad way! Lottie Jones—she's on nights in the Accident Room, she says they've broken every bone in their bodies.'

Deborah was putting out the sharps and needles and collecting the electrical equipment. 'In which case we're going to be here for a very long time,' she remarked cheerfully. 'Where's Nurse Patterson?'

That young lady, only half awake, crept through the door as she put the question, wished her superior a sleepy good morning and went on to say: 'They're mincemeat, Sister, so rumour has it, and where's the night staff? Couldn't they have at least started...?'

'It's not only our three,' Deborah pointed out crisply. 'They've had a busy night, the general theatre has been on the go since midnight. Get the plaster room ready, will you, Nurse, and then see to the bowls.'

She was on the point of scrubbing up ready to start her trolleys when Mr van Doorninck walked in. She looked at him twice, because she was accustomed to seeing him either in his theatre gown and trousers, or a selection of sober, beautifully cut grey suits, and now he was in slacks and a rather elderly sweater. It made him look younger and much more approachable and it seemed to have the same effect on him as well, for he said cheerfully, 'Hullo—sorry we had to get you up early, but I wanted you here. Do you suppose they could send up some coffee—I can tell you what I intend doing while we drink it.' He glanced around him. 'These three look as though they could do with a hot drink, too,' a remark which sent Patterson scurrying to the telephone to order coffee in the consultant's name, adding a gleeful rider that it was for five people and was to be sent up at once.

Deborah led the way to her office, offered Mr van Doorninck a chair, which he declined, and sat down herself behind her desk. She had taken off her cap and had her theatre cap and mask in her hand, but she put these down now and rather absent-mindedly began to thrust the pins more securely into the great bundle of hair she had twisted up in such a hurry. She did it with a lack of self-consciousness of which she was unaware and when she looked up and caught his eye, she said, 'Sorry about this—there wasn't much time, but I'm listening.'

'Three cases,' he began. 'The first is a young man —a boy, I should say, fractured pelvis, left and right fractured femurs, I'm afraid, and a fractured patella—fragmented, I shall have to remove the whole thing. The other two aren't quite so bad—fractured neck of femur, compound tib and fib and a few ribs; the third one has got off comparatively lightly with a comminuted fracture of left femur and a Potts'. I think if we work the first case off, stop for a quick breakfast, and get the other two done afterwards—have you a list for Mr Squires this morning? Doesn't he usually start at eleven o'clock?'

Deborah nodded. 'But it's a short list and I'm sure he'll agree to start half an hour later if he were asked.'

'How are you placed for staff? Will you be able to cover both theatres? You'll be running late.'

It was Staff's half day before her days off, but he wouldn't know about that. Deborah said positively: 'I can manage very well; Bob will be on at eight o'clock and both part-time staff nurses come in.'

She made a show of consulting the off-duty book before her. She wouldn't be able to go off duty herself, for she was to be relieved by one of the part-time staff nurses; she would have to telephone her now, and get her to come in at one o'clock instead.

'When would you like to start?' she wanted to know calmly.

He glanced at his watch. 'Ten minutes, if you can.'

She got up from her chair. 'We'll be ready—you'll want the Smith–Petersen nails, and shall I put out the McLaughlin pin-plate as well? And will you want to do a bone graft on the tib and fib?'

'Very probably. Put out everything we've got, will you? I'll pick what I want, we can't really assess the damage until I can get the bone fragments away.'

He followed her out of the office and they walked together down the wide corridor to the scrubbing-up room, where Peter was already at one of the basins. Deborah wished him good morning and went to her own basin to scrub—ten minutes wasn't long and she had quite a lot to do still.

The operation lasted for hours, and unlike other jobs, there was no question of hurrying it up; the broken bones had to be exposed, tidied up, blood vessels tied, tissue cut away and then the pieces brought together before they were joined by means of pins or wires, and only then after they had been X-rayed.

Mr van Doorninck worked steadily and with the absorption of a man doing a difficult jigsaw puzzle. oblivious of time or anything else. Deborah, with an eye on the clock, sent a nurse down to breakfast with the whispered warning to look sharp about it; Staff went next and when Bob came on at eight o'clock and with him the other two student nurses, she breathed more freely. She still had to telephone Mrs Rudge, the part-time staff nurse, but she lived close by and with any luck she would be able to change her duty hours; she would worry about that later. She nodded to Bob to be ready with the drill, checked swabs with the junior nurse, and tidied her trolleys.

The case was wheeled away at long last, and as the patient disappeared through one door, Mr van Doorninck and Peter started off in the opposite direction. 'Twenty minutes?' said Mr van Doorninck over his shoulder as he went, not waiting for her reply.

'You must be joking,' Deborah muttered crossly, and picked up a handful of instruments, to freeze into immobility as he stopped abruptly. 'You're right, of course—is half an hour better?'

She said 'Yes, sir,' in a small meek voice and plunged into the ordered maelstrom which was the theatre. Twenty minutes later she was in her office, her theatre cap pushed to the back of her head, drinking the tea Staff had whistled up for her and wolfing down buttered toast; heaven knew when she would get her next meal....

She certainly didn't get it at dinnertime, for although the second case proved plain sailing, even if slow, the third presented every small complication under the sun; the femur was in fragments, anyone less sure of himself than Mr van Doorninck might have felt justified in amputating below the knee, but he, having made up his mind that he could save the limb, set to work to do so, and a long and tedious business it was, necessitating Deborah sending Mrs Rudge to the second theatre to take care of Mr Squires who had obligingly agreed to take his list there, and she had taken two of the nurses with her, a circumstance which had caused Staff Nurse Perkins to hesitate about taking her half day, but it was impossible to argue about it in theatre; she

17

went, reluctantly.

The operation lasted another hour. Deborah had contrived to send the nurses to their dinners, but Bob she didn't dare to send; he was far too useful and understood the electric drills and the diathermy machine even better than she did herself—besides, she was scrubbed, and at this stage of the operation there was no question of hampering Mr van Doorninck for a single second.

It was half past two when he finally straightened his back, thanked her politely for her services and walked away. She sent Bob to his belated dinner, and when Mrs Rudge arrived from the other theatre, went downstairs herself to cold beef and salad. There was certainly no hope of off-duty for her now. Mrs Rudge would go at four o'clock and that would leave herself and two student nurses when Bob went at five. She sighed, eating almost nothing, and presently went over to the Nurses' Home and tidied herself in a perfunctory manner, a little horrified at the untidiness of her appearance—luckily it had all been hidden under her cap and mask.

It had just turned four o'clock when the Accident Room telephoned to say that there was a small child coming up within minutes with a nasty compound fracture of upper arm. Deborah raced round collecting instruments, scrubbing to lay the trolley while telling the nurses, a little fearful at having to get on with it without Staff to breathe reassuringly down their necks, what to do next. All the same, they did so well that she was behind her trolley, scrubbed and threading needles when the patient was wheeled in, followed by Mr van Doorninck and Peter.

'Oh,' said Deborah, taken delightfully by surprise, 'I didn't know that it would be you, sir.'

'I was in the building, Sister,' he informed her, and accepted the towel clip she was holding out. 'You have been off duty?'

She passed him a scalpel. 'No.'

'You will be going this evening?'

She took the forceps off the Mayo table and held them ready for Peter to take. 'No,' then added hastily, in case he should think she was vexed about it, 'It doesn't matter in the least.'

He said 'Um' behind his mask and didn't speak again during the operation, which went without a hitch. All the same, it was almost six o'clock when they were finished and it would be another hour before the theatre was restored to its pristine state. It was a great pity that Peter had to put a plaster on a Potts' fracture—it was a simple one and he did it in the little plaster room, but he made a good deal of mess and Deborah, squeezing out plaster bandages in warm water for him to wind round the broken leg, found her temper wearing thin. It had been a long day, she was famished and tired and she must look a sight by now and there were still the books to write up. She glanced at the clock. In ten minutes the nurses were due off duty; she would have to stay and do her writing before she closed the theatre. She sighed and Peter cocked an eyebrow at her and asked: 'Worn out, Deb?'

'Not really, just hungry, and I haven't had time to do my hair properly or see to my face all day. I feel a fright.' She could hear her voice sounding cross, but he ignored it and agreed cheerfully:

'You look pretty awful—luckily you're so gorgeous, it doesn't matter, though the hair is a trifle wild.'

She giggled and slapped a wet bandage into his outstretched hand.

'Well, it doesn't matter, there's no one to see me. I shall eat an enormous supper and fall into bed.'

'Lucky girl—I'm on until midnight.'

She was instantly sympathetic. 'Oh, Peter, how awful, but there's not much of a list for Mr Squires tomorrow afternoon and only a handful of re-plasters and walking irons—you might be able to get someone to give you a hand.'

He nodded. 'We're on call, aren't we?'

That was true; Clare's was on call until Thursday. 'I'll keep my fingers crossed,' she promised him. 'And now be off with you, I want to clear up.'

It was very quiet when the nurses had gone. Deborah tugged her cap off her dreadfully untidy hair, kicked off her shoes, and sat down at her desk. Another ten minutes or so and she would be free herself. She dragged her thoughts away from the tantalising prospect of supper and a hot bath and set to on the operation book. She was neatly penning in the last name when the unit doors swung open and her tired mind registered the disturbing fact that it was Mr van Doorninck's large feet coming down the corridor, and she looking like something the sea had washed up. She was still frantically searching for her shoes when he came in the door. She rose to her stockinged feet, feeling even worse than she looked because he was, by contrast, quite immaculate—no one, looking at him now, would know that he had been bent over the operating table for the entire day. He didn't look tired either; his handsome face, with its straight nose and firm mouth, looked as good-humoured and relaxed as it usually did.

Deborah spoke her thoughts aloud and quite involuntarily. 'Oh, dear—I wasn't expecting anyone and I simply....' She broke off because he was smiling nicely at her. 'I must look quite awful,' she muttered, and when he laughed softly: 'Is it another case?' He shook his head. 'You want to borrow some instruments—half a minute while I find my shoes....'

He laughed again. 'You won't need your shoes and I don't want any instruments.' He came a little further into the room and stood looking at her. She looked back at him, bewildered, her mind noting that his Dutch accent seemed more pronounced than usual although his English was faultless.

'How do you feel about marrying me?' he wanted to know blandly.

CHAPTER TWO

SHE was so amazed that she couldn't speak. Just for one blissful moment she savoured the delightful idea that he had fallen in love with her, and then common sense took over. Men in love, however awkward about the business, weren't likely to employ such a cool manner as his. He had sounded for all the world as though he wanted her to fit in an extra case on his next list or something equally prosaic. She found her voice at last and was surprised at its steadiness. 'Why do you ask me?' she wanted to know.

She watched his nod of approval. The light over the desk showed up the grey hair at his temples and served to highlight the extreme fairness of the rest.

His voice was unhurried as he said pleasantly:

'What a sensible girl you are—most women would have been demanding to know if I were joking. I have noticed your calm manner when we have worked together, and I am delighted to see that it isn't only in the operating theatre that you are unflurried.'

He was silent for so long that Deborah, desperate for something, anything to do, sat down again and began to stack the various notebooks and papers neatly together. That there was no need to do this, and indeed it would merely give her more work in the morning sorting them all out again, escaped her notice. He might think her sensible and calm; inside, happily concealed by her dark blue uniform, she was bubbling like a cauldron on the boil.

Presently, in the same pleasant voice, he went on: 'I will explain. I am returning to Holland to live very shortly; my father died recently and it is necessary for me to live there—there are various obligations——' he dismissed them with a wave of his hand and she wondered what they might be. 'I shall continue with my work, naturally, but we are a large family and I have a great many friends, so there will be entertaining and social occasions, you understand. I have neither the time nor the inclination to arrange such things, neither do I have the slightest idea how to run a household. I need a wife, someone who will do these things and welcome my friends.'

He paused, but she wasn't looking at him. There were some retractors on the desk, put there for repair; she had picked them up and was polishing their handles vigorously with the cloth in which they were wrapped. He leaned across the desk and took them from her without a word and went on: 'I should tell you that I have been married. My wife died eight years ago and I have had no wish to become deeply involved with any woman since; I do not want to become deeply involved with you, but I see very little likelihood of this; we have worked together now for two years and I believe that I understand you very well. I would wish for your companionship and friendship and nothing more. I am aware that women set great store by marrying for love and that they are frequently unhappy as a consequence. Perhaps you do not consider what I am offering enough, and yet it seems to me that we are ideally suited, for you have plenty of common sense, a delightful manner and, I think, similar tastes to my own. I can promise you that your life will be pleasant enough.' His blue eyes stared down at her from under half-closed lids. 'You're twenty-seven,' he told her, 'and pretty enough to have had several chances of marrying and settling down with a husband and children, but you have not wanted this—am I right?'

She nodded wordlessly, squashing a fleeting, non-sensical dream of little flaxen-haired van Doornincks as soon as it had been born. Because she simply had to know, she asked: 'Have you any children?'

'No,' his voice was so remote that she wished she hadn't spoken, 'I have two brothers and a sister, all married—there are children enough in the family.'

Deborah waited for him to ask her if she liked children, but he didn't, so after a minute or two's silence she said in a quiet little voice:

'May I have some time to think about it? You see, I've always imagined that I would marry someone I...' She stopped because she wasn't sure of her voice any more.

'Loved?' he finished for her in a depressingly matter-of-fact tone. 'I imagine most girls do, but I think that is not always the best way. A liking for each other, consideration for one's partner, shared interests—these things make a good marriage.'

She stared at him, her lovely eyes round. She hadn't supposed him to be a cold man, although he was talking like one now. Either he had been unhappy in his first marriage or he had loved his wife so dearly that the idea of loving any other woman was unthinkable to him. She found either possibility unsatisfactory. With a tremendous effort she made herself be as businesslike as he was. 'So you don't want children—or—or a wife?'

He smiled. 'Shall we discuss that later? Perhaps I haven't made myself quite plain; I admire and like you, but I'm not in love with you and I believe that we can be happy together. We are sensible, mature people and you are not, I believe, a romantic girl....'

She longed to tell him how wrong he was. Instead: 'You don't believe in falling in love, then?'

He smiled so charmingly that her outraged heart cracked a little.

'And nor, I think, do you, Deborah, otherwise you would have been married long ago—you must be single from choice.'

So that was what he thought; that she cared nothing for marriage and children and a home of her own. She kept her angry eyes on the desk and said nothing at all.

Presently he said, 'I have offended you. I'm sorry, but I find myself quite unable to be anything

24

but honest with you.'

She looked up at that and encountered his blue stare. 'I've had chances to marry,' she told him, at the same time wondering what would happen if she told him just why she had given up those same chances. 'Did you love your wife?' The question had popped out before she had been able to stop it and she watched the bleak look on his face as it slowly chilled her.

He said with a bitter little sneer which hurt her, 'All women are curious. . . .'

'Well, I'm not all women,' she assured him sharply, 'and I'm not in the least curious'—another lie—'but it's something I should have to know— you said you wanted to be honest.'

He looked at her thoughtfully. 'You're quite right. One day we will talk about her. Will it suffice for the moment if I tell you that our marriage was a mistake?' He became his usual slightly reserved self again. 'Now that I have told you so much about myself, I do not see that you can do anything else but marry me.'

She answered his smile and was tempted to say yes at once, but common sense still had a firm place inside her lovely head; she would have to think about it. She told him so and he agreed unconcernedly. 'I shall see you on Thursday,' he observed as he went to the door. 'I'll leave you to finish your writing. Good night, Deborah.'

She achieved a calm 'Good night, Mr van Doorninck,' and he paused on the way out to say: 'My name is Gerard, by the way, but perhaps I shouldn't have told you that until Thursday.'

Deborah did no more writing; she waited until she heard the swing doors close after him and then shovelled the books and papers into a drawer, pell-mell. They could wait until tomorrow—she had far too much on her mind to be bothered with stupid matters like off-duty and laundry and instruments which needed repairing. She pinned on her cap anyhow, found her shoes at last, locked the theatre, hung the keys on the hook above the door, and went down to supper. Several of her friends were as late as she was; they greeted her with tired good nature and broke into a babble of talk to which she didn't listen until the Accident Room Sister start-led her by saying, 'Deb, whatever is the matter? I've asked you at least three times what van Door-ninck did with those three cases we sent up, and you just sit there in a world of your own.'

'Sorry,' said Deborah, 'I was thinking,' a remark which called forth a little ripple of weary laughter from everyone at the table. She smiled round at them all and plunged obligingly into the com-plexities of the three patients' operations.

'No off-duty?' someone asked when she had fin-ished.

Deborah shook her head. 'No—I'll make it up some time.'

'He works you too hard,' said a pretty dark girl from the other side of the table. 'Cunning wretch, I suppose he turned on the charm and you fell for it.'

The Accident Room Sister said half-jokingly, 'And what wouldn't you give to have the chance of doing just that, my girl? The handsome Mr van Doorninck is a confirmed bachelor, to the sorrow of us all, and the only reason Deb has lasted so long in theatre is because she never shows the least in-terest in him, so he feels safe with her. Isn't that right, Deb?'

Deborah blushed seldom; by a great effort of will she prevented herself from doing so now. She agreed airily, her fingers crossed on her lap, and started on the nourishing rice pudding which had been set before her. She wouldn't have rice pudding, she promised herself. Perhaps the Dutch ... she pulled her thoughts up sharply; she hadn't decided yet, had she? It would be ridiculous to accept his offer, for it wouldn't be the kind of marriage she would want in the first place, on the other hand there was the awful certainty that if she refused him she would never see him again, which meant that she would either remain single all her days or marry someone else without loving him. So wasn't it better to marry Mr van Doorninck even if he didn't love her? At least she would be with him for the rest of her life and he need never find out that she loved him; he hadn't discovered it so far, so why should he later on?

She spooned the last of the despised pudding, and decided to marry him, and if she had regrets in the years to come she would only have herself to blame. It was a relief to have made up her mind, although perhaps it had been already made up from the very moment when he had startled her with his proposal, for hadn't it been the fulfilment of her wildest dreams?

She retired to her room early on the plea of a hard day and the beginnings of a headache, determined to go to bed and think the whole preposterous idea over rationally. Instead of which she fell sound asleep within a few minutes of putting her head on the pillow, her thoughts an uncontrollable and delicious jumble.

27

She had time enough to think the next day, though. Wednesday was always a slack day in theatre even though they had to be prepared for emergencies. But there were no lists; Deborah spent the greater part of the day in the office, catching up on the administrative side, only sallying forth from time to time to make sure that the nurses knew what they were about. She went off duty at five o'clock, secretly disappointed that Mr van Doorninck hadn't put in an appearance—true, he hadn't said that he would, but surely he would feel some impatience? Upon reflection she decided that probably he wouldn't, or if he did, he would take care not to let it show. She spent the evening washing her hair and doing her nails, with the vague idea that she needed to look her best when he arrived at ten o'clock the next morning.

Only he didn't come at ten. She was in theatre, on her knees under the operating table because one of the nurses had reported a small fault in its mechanism. She had her back to the door and didn't hear him enter; it was the sight of his large well-polished shoes which caused her to start up, knocking her cap crooked as she did so. He put out a hand and helped her to her feet without effort, rather as though she had been some small slip of a girl, and Deborah exclaimed involuntarily, 'Oh— I'm quite heavy. I'm too tall, you must have noticed.' Her eyes were on his tie as she babbled on: 'I'm so big . . .!'

'Which should make us a well-suited couple,' he answered equably. 'At least, I hope you will agree with me, Deborah.'

She put a hand up to her cap to straighten it, not quite sure what she should answer, and he caught her puzzled look. 'Not quite romantic enough?' he quizzed her gently. 'Have dinner with me tonight and I'll try and make amends.'

She was standing before him now, her lovely eyes on a level with his chin. 'I don't know—that is, I haven't said . . .'

His heavy-lidded eyes searched hers. 'Then say it now,' he commanded her gently. It seemed absurd to accept a proposal of marriage in an operating theatre, but there seemed no help for it. She drew breath:

'Yes, I'll marry you, Mr van Doorninck.' She uttered the absurd remark in a quiet, sensible voice and he laughed gently.

'Gerard, don't you think? Can you manage seven o'clock?'

Her eyes left his chin reluctantly and met his. 'Yes, I think so.'

'Good. I'll fetch you—we'll go to the Empress if you would like that.'

Somewhere very super, she remembered vaguely. 'That will be nice.' An inadequate answer, she knew, but he didn't appear to find it amiss; he took her two hands lightly in his and said: 'We'll have a quiet talk together—it is essential that we should understand each other from the beginning, don't you agree?'

It sounded very businesslike and cool to her; perhaps she was making a terrible mistake, but was there a worse mistake than letting him go away for ever? She thought not. For want of anything better to say, she repeated, 'That will be nice,' and added, 'I must go and scrub, you have a list as long as your arm.'

It stretched longer than an arm, however, by the

time they had finished. The second case held them
up; the patient's unexpected cardiac arrest was a
surprise which, while to be coped with, flung a decided spanner in the works. Not that Mr van Doorninck allowed it to impede his activities—he con-
tinued unhurriedly about his urgent business and
Deborah, after despatching Staff to the other end of
the table to help the anaesthetist in any way he
wished, concentrated upon supplying her future
husband's wants. The patient rallied, she heard Mr
van Doorninck's satisfied grunt and relaxed herself;
for a patient to die on the table was something to
be avoided at all costs. The operation was con-
cluded and the patient, still unconscious and happily unaware of his frustrated attempts to die, was
borne away and it was decided that a break for
coffee would do everyone some good. Deborah,
crowding into her office with the three men and
sharing the contents of the coffee pot with them,
was less lucky with the biscuit tin, for it was emp-
tied with a rapidity she wouldn't have prevented
even if she could have done so; the sight of grown
men munching Rich Tea biscuits as though they
had eaten nothing for days touched her heart. She
poured herself a second cup of coffee and made a
mental note to wheedle the stores into letting her
have an extra supply.

The rest of the morning went well, although
they finished more than an hour late. Mr van
Doorninck was meticulously drawing the muscle
sheath together, oblivious of time. He lifted an
eyebrow at Peter to remove the clamps and swab
the wound ready for him to stitch and put out an
outsize gloved hand for the needleholder which
Deborah was holding ready. He took it without a

glance and paused to straighten his back. 'Anything for this afternoon, Sister?' he enquired conversationally.

'Not until three o'clock, sir.' She glanced at Peter, who would be taking the cases. 'A baby for a gallows frame and a couple of Colles.'

'So you will be free for our evening together?'

'Yes, sir.' Hadn't she already said so? she asked herself vexedly, and threaded another needle, aware of the pricked ears and held breaths around her and Peter's swift, astonished look.

Mr van Doorninck held out his needleholder for her to insert the newly threaded needle. He said deliberately so that everyone could hear, 'Sister Culpeper and I are engaged to be married, so we are—er—celebrating this evening.'

He put out a hand again and Deborah slapped the stitch scissors into it with a certain amount of force, her fine bosom swelling with annoyance— giving out the news like that without so much as a word to her beforehand! Just wait until we're alone, she cautioned him silently, her smouldering look quite lost upon his downbent, intent head. And even if she had wanted to speak her mind, it would have been impossible in the little chorus of good wishes and congratulations. She made suitable murmurs in reply and scowled behind her mask.

But if she had hoped to have had a few words with him she was unlucky; the patient was no sooner stitched than he threw down his instruments, ripped off his gloves and made off with the long, leisurely stride which could only have been matched on her part by a frank run. She watched him go, fuming, and turned away to fob off the nurses' excited questions.

Her temper had improved very little by the time she went off duty. The news had spread, as such news always did; she was telephoned, stopped in the corridors and beseiged by the other Sisters when she went down to tea. That they were envious was obvious, but they were pleased too, for she was well liked at Clare's, and each one of them marvelled at the way she had kept the exciting news such a close secret.

'He'll be a honey,' sighed Women's Surgical Sister. 'Just imagine living with him!' She stared at Deborah. 'Is he very rich, Deb?'

'I—I don't really know.' Deborah was by now quite peevish and struggling not to show it. It was a relief, on the pretext of dressing up for the evening, when she could escape. All the same, despite her ill-humour, she dressed with care in a pinafore dress of green ribbed silk, worn over a white lawn blouse with ballooning sleeves and a fetching choirboy frill under her chin, and she did her hair carefully too, its smooth wings on her cheeks and the complicated chignon at the back of her neck setting off the dress to its greatest advantage. Luckily it was late August and warm, for she had no suitable coat to cover this finery; she rummaged around in her cupboard and found a gossamer wool scarf which she flung over her arm—and if he didn't like it, she told her reflection crossly, he could lump it.

Still buoyed up by indignation, she swept down the Home stairs, looking queenly and still slightly peevish, but she stopped in full sail in the hall because Mr van Doorninck was there, standing by the door, watching her. He crossed the polished floor and when he reached her said the wrong thing. 'I had no idea,' he commented, 'that you were such a handsome young woman.'

His words conjured up an outsize, tightly cor-
seted Titanic, when her heart's wish was to be frail
and small and clinging. She lifted pansy eyes to his
and said tartly, 'My theatre gowns are a good dis-
guise....' and stopped because she could see that he
was laughing silently.

'I beg your pardon, Deborah—you see how necessary it is for me to take a wife? I have become so
inept at paying compliments. I like you exactly as
you are and I hope that you will believe that. But
tell me, why were you looking so put out as you
came downstairs?'

She felt mollified and a little ashamed too. 'I was
annoyed because you told everyone in theatre that
we were engaged—I didn't know you were going
to.'

He chose to misunderstand her. 'I had no idea
that you wished it to remain a secret.' He smiled so
nicely at her that her heart hurried its beat.

'Well—of course I didn't.'

'Then why were you annoyed?'

An impossible question to answer. She smiled reluctantly and said:

'Oh, I don't know—perhaps I haven't quite got
used to the idea.'

His blue eyes searched hers calmly. 'You have
had second thoughts, perhaps?'

'No—oh, no.'

He smiled again. 'Good. Shall we go?'

They went through the Home door together,
and she was very conscious of the unseen eyes peer-
ing at them from the net-covered windows, but she
forgot all about them when she saw the car drawn
up waiting for them. She had wondered from time

to time what sort of car he drove, and here it was—
a BMW 3 OCSL, a sleek, powerful coupé which
looked as though it could do an enormous speed if
it were allowed to. She paused by its door and
asked: 'Yours?'

'Yes. I could use a larger car really, but once I'm
in it it's O.K., and she goes like a bird. We'll
change her, though, if you prefer something room-
ier.'

Deborah had settled herself in her seat. 'She's
super, you mustn't dream of changing her.' She
turned to look at him as he got in beside her. 'I
always imagined that you would drive something
stately.'

He laughed. 'I'm flattered that you spared even
such thoughts as those upon me. I've a Citroën at
home, an SM, plenty of room but not so fast as this
one. I take it that you drive?'

He had eased the car into the evening traffic and
was travelling westward. 'Well,' said Deborah, 'I
drive, but I'm not what you would call a good
driver, though I haven't had much opportunity....'

'Then we must find opportunity for you—you
will need a car of your own.'

In Piccadilly, where the traffic was faster and
thinner, he turned off into Berkeley Street and
stopped outside the Empress Restaurant. A truly
imposing place, she discovered, peeping discreetly
about her as they went in—grandly Victorian with
its red plush and its candelabra. When they were
seated she said with disarming frankness: 'It rather
takes my breath away.'

His mouth twitched. 'Worthy of the occasion, I
hope.' He opened his eyes wide and she was surprised, as she always was, by their intense blue. 'For

34

it is an occasion, is it not?'

She studied him; he was really extraordinarily handsome and very distinguished in his dinner jacket. After a moment he said softly:

'I hope I pass muster?'

She blinked and smiled rather shyly. 'I beg your pardon—I didn't mean to stare. It's just that—well, you never see a person properly in theatre, do you?'

He studied her in his turn. 'No—and I made a mistake just now. I called you handsome, and you're not, you're beautiful.'

She flushed delicately under his gaze and he went on blandly: 'But let us make no mistake, I'm not getting sentimental or falling in love with you, Deborah.' His voice had a faint edge which she was quick to hear.

She forced her own voice to normality. 'You explained about that, but supposing you should meet someone with whom you do fall in love? And you might, you're not old, are you?'

'I'm thirty-seven,' he informed her, still bland, 'and I have had a number of years in which to fall in and out of love since Sasja's death.' He saw her look and smiled slightly. 'And by that I mean exactly what I said; I must confess I've been attracted to a number of women, but I didn't like them—there is a difference. I like you, Deborah.'

She sipped the drink he had ordered and studied the menu card and tried not to mind too much that he was talking to her as though she were an old friend who had just applied for a job he had going. In a way she was. She put the idea out of her head and chose Suprême de Turbot Mogador and settled for caviare for starters, then applied herself to a lighthearted conversation which gave him no opportunity of turning the talk back to themselves. But that didn't last long; with the coming of the Vacherin Glacé he cut easily into her flow of small talk with:

'As to our marriage—have you any objection if it takes place soon? I want to return to Holland as quickly as possible and I have arranged to leave Clare's in ten days' time. I thought we might get married then.'

Deborah sat with her fork poised midway between plate and mouth. 'Ten days' time?' she uttered. 'But that's not possible! I have to give a month's notice.'

'Oh, don't concern yourself with that. I can arrange something. Is that your only objection?'

'You don't know my family.'

'You live in Somerset, don't you? We might go down there and see them before we go to Holland —unless you wish to be married from your home?'

It was like being swept along a fast-moving river with not even a twig in sight. 'I—I hadn't thought about it.'

'Then how would it be if we marry quietly here in London and then go to see your parents?'

'You mean surprise them?'

'I'll be guided by you,' he murmured.

She thought this rather unlikely; all the same it was a good idea.

'Father's an historian,' she explained, 'and rather wrapped up in his work, and Mother—Mother is never surprised about anything. They wouldn't mind. I'd like a quiet wedding, but in church.'

He looked surprised. 'Naturally. I am a Calvinist myself and you are presumably Church of England.

If you care to choose your church I'll see about the licence and make the arrangements. Do you want any guests?'

She shook her head; it didn't seem quite right to invite people to a marriage which was, after all, a friendly arrangement between two people who were marrying for all the wrong reasons—although there was nothing wrong with her reason; surely loving someone was sufficiently strong grounds for marrying them? And as for Gerard, his reasons, though very different, held a strong element of practical common sense. Besides, he believed her to be in complete agreement with him over the suitability of a marriage between two persons who, presumably, had no intention of allowing their hearts to run away with their feelings. She wondered idly just what kind of a girl might steal his heart. Certainly not herself—had he not said that he liked her, and that, as far as she could see, was as far as it went.

She drank her coffee and agreed with every show of pleasure to his suggestion that they should go somewhere and dance.

He took her to the Savoy, where they danced for an hour or more between pleasant little interludes at the table he had secured well away from the dance floor. She was an excellent dancer and Gerard, she discovered, danced well too, if a trifle conservatively. Just for a space she forgot her problems and gave herself to the enjoyment of the evening, and presently, drinking champagne, her face prettily flushed, she found herself agreeing that a light supper would be delightful before he took her back to Clare's. It was almost three o'clock when he stopped the car outside the Home. He got out of the car with her and opened the heavy door with the latch key she gave him and then stood idly swinging it in his hand.

'Thank you for a delightful evening,' said Deborah, and tried to remember that she was going to marry this large, quiet man standing beside her, and in ten days, too. She felt sudden panic swamp the tenuous happiness inspired by the champagne and the dancing, and raised her eyes to his face, her mouth already open to give utterance to a variety of thoughts which, largely because of that same champagne, no longer made sense.

The eyes which met hers were very kind. 'Don't worry, Deborah,' he urged her in his deep, placid voice. 'It's only reaction; in the morning everything will be quite all right again. You must believe me.'

He bent and kissed her cheek, much as though he were comforting a child, and told her to go to bed. 'And I'll see you tomorrow before I go to Holland.'

And because she was bewildered and a little afraid and her head had begun to ache, she did as he bade her. With a whispered good night she went slowly up the stairs without looking back to see if he was watching her, undressed and got into bed, and fell at once into a dreamless sleep which was only ended by her alarm clock warning her to get up and dress, astonished to find that what Gerard had said was quite true; everything did seem all right. She went down to breakfast and in response to the urgent enquiries of her companions, gave a detailed account of her evening and then, fortified by several cups of strong tea, made her way to the theatre unit.

There wasn't much doing. Mr Squires had a couple of Smith–Petersen pins to insert, a bone graft to do, and there was a Carpal Tunnel—an easy enough list, for he kept strictly to straightforward bone work, leaving the bone tumours to Gerard van Doorninck. They were finished by one o'clock and Deborah had time to go down to dinner before sending Staff off duty. The theatre would have to be washed down that afternoon and she wanted to go through the sharps; some of the chisels needed attention, as did the grooved awl and one or two of the rugines. She would go down to the surgical stores and see what could be done. She had them neatly wrapped and was on the point of making her way through the labyrinth of semiunderground passages to the stores, when Gerard walked in. 'Hullo,' he said. 'Going somewhere?'

She explained about the sharps, and even as she was speaking he had taken them from her and put them on the desk. 'Later. I have to go again in a few minutes. I just wanted to make sure....' he paused and studied her with cool leisure. Apparently her calm demeanour pleased him, for he said: 'I told you that everything would be all right, didn't I?' and when she nodded, longing to tell him that indeed nothing was right at all, he went on: 'I've seen about the licence—there's a small church round the corner, St Joram's. Would you like to go and see it and tell me if you will marry me there?'

Her heart jumped because she still wasn't used to the idea of marrying him, although her face remained tranquil enough. 'I know St Joram's very well, I go there sometimes. I should like to be married there.'

He gave a small satisfied sound, like a man who had had a finicky job to do and had succeeded with it sooner than he had expected.

'I'll be back on Monday—there's a list at ten o'clock, isn't there? I'll see you before we start.'

He took her hand briefly, said goodbye even more briefly, and retraced his steps. Deborah stood in the empty corridor, listening to his unhurried stride melt into the distance and then merge into the multitude of hospital sounds. Presently she picked up the instruments and started on her way to the surgical stores.

CHAPTER THREE

THE warmth of the early September morning had barely penetrated the dim cool of the little church. Deborah, standing in its porch, peered down its length; in a very few minutes she was going to walk down the aisle with Gerard beside her and become his wife. She wished suddenly that he hadn't left her there while he returned to lock the car parked outside, because then she wouldn't have time to think. Now her head seethed with the events of the last ten days; the interview with Miss Bright, the Principal Nursing Officer, and the astonishing ease with which she found herself free to leave exactly when Gerard had wanted her to; the delight and curiosity of her friends, who even at that very moment had no idea that she was getting married this very morning; she had allowed them to think that she and Gerard were going down to her parents in Somerset. She had even allowed them to discuss her wedding dress, with a good deal of friendly bickering as to which style and material would suit her best, and had quietly gone out and shopped around for a pale blue dress and jacket and a wisp of a hat which she had only put on in the car, in case someone in the hospital should have seen it and guessed what it might be, for it was that sort of a hat. But the hat was the only frivolous thing about her; she looked completely composed, and when she heard Gerard's step behind her, she turned a tranquil face to greet him, very much at variance with her heart's secret thudding.

He had flowers in his hand, a small spray of roses and orange blossom and green leaves. 'For you,' he said. 'I know that you should have a bouquet, but it might have been difficult to hide from your friends.' He spoke easily with no sign of discomposure and proceeded to fasten them on to her dress in a matter-of-fact manner. When he had done so, he stood back to look at her. 'Very nice,' was his verdict. 'How lucky that we have such a glorious morning.' He looked at his watch. 'We're a few minutes early, shall we stroll round the church?'

They wandered off, examining the memorials on the walls and the gravestones at their feet, for all the world, thought Deborah, slightly light-headed, as though they were a pair of tourists. It was when they reached the pulpit that she noticed the flowers beautifully arranged around the chancel. She stopped before one particularly fine mass of blooms and remarked: 'How beautiful these are, and so many of them. I shouldn't have thought that the parish was rich enough to afford anything like this.'

She turned to look at her companion as she spoke and exclaimed:

'Oh, you had them put here. How—how thought-ful!'

'I'm glad you like them. I found the church a little bare when I came the other day—the vicar's wife was only too glad to see to them for me.'

'Thank you,' said Deborah. She touched the flowers on her dress. 'And for these too.'

They had reached the chancel at exactly the right moment; the vicar was waiting for them with two people—his wife, apparently, and someone who might have been the daily help, pressed into the more romantic role of witness.

The service was short. Deborah listened to every word of it and heard nothing, and even when the plain gold ring had been put upon her finger she felt as though it was someone else standing there, being married. She signed the register in a composed manner, received her husband's kiss with the same calm, and shook hands with the vicar and the two ladies, then walked out of the little church with Gerard. He was holding her hand lightly, talking quietly as they went, and she said not a word, only noticed every small detail about him— his grey suit, the gold cuff links in his silk shirt, the perfection of his polished shoes—who polished them? she wondered stupidly—and his imperturbable face. He turned to smile at her as they reached the door and she smiled back while hope, reinforced by her love, flooded through her. She was young still and pretty, some said beautiful, men liked her, some enough to have wanted to marry her; surely there was a chance that Gerard might fall in love with her? She would be seeing much more of him now, take an interest in his life, make herself indispensable, wear pretty clothes. . . .

'My dear girl,' said Gerard kindly, 'how distraite you have become—quite lost in thought—happy ones, I hope?'

They were standing by the car and he had unlocked the door as he spoke and was holding it open for her, his glance as kind as his voice. She got in, strangely vexed by his kindness, and said too brightly: 'It was a nice wedding. I—I was thinking about it.'

He nodded and swung the car into the street. 'Yes, one hears the words during a simple ceremony —I have always thought that big social weddings are slightly unreal.'

It was on the tip of her tongue to ask him if his previous wedding had been just such a one, but it seemed hardly a fitting time to do so. She launched into a steady flow of small talk which lasted until they were clear of the centre of the city and heading west.

But presently she fell silent, staring out at the passing traffic as the car gathered speed, casting around in her mind for something to talk about. There was so much to say, and yet nothing. She was on the point of remarking—for the second time— about the weather when Gerard spoke. 'I think we'll lunch at Nately Scures—there's a good pub there, the Baredown. I don't know about you, Deborah, but getting married seems to have given me a good appetite.'

His manner was so completely at ease that she lost her awkwardness too. 'I'm hungry too,' she agreed, 'and I didn't realise that it was already one o'clock. We should be home by tea time.'

It was during lunch that one or two notions, not altogether pleasant, entered her head and quite unknown to her, reflected their disquiet in her face. They were sitting back at their ease, drinking their coffee in a companionable silence which Gerard broke. 'What's on your mind, Deborah?'

She put some more sugar into her cup although she didn't want it, and stirred it because it gave her something to do. She began uncertainly: 'I was just thinking—hoping that Mike, my elder brother, you know, will be home for a day or two with Helen—his wife.'

He smiled very faintly. 'Why?'

'Well, I was thinking about—about rooms. You see, the house is very old and there aren't....' She tried again. 'There is Mother and Father's room and a big guest room, all the other bedrooms are small. If Mike and Helen are there they'll be in the guest room, which makes it easy for us, because then we shall have our own rooms and there won't be any need for me to make an excuse—I mean for us not sharing a room.' She gave him a determinedly matter-of-fact look which he returned with an urbane one of his own. 'I don't suppose you had thought about it?'

'Indeed I had—I thought a migraine would fill the bill.'

'Do you have migraine?'

'Good God, girl, no! You.'

She said indignantly: 'I've never had migraine in my life, I don't even know what it feels like. I really don't think....'

He gave her an amused glance. 'Well, it seems the situation isn't likely to arise, doesn't it? We can hardly turn your brother and his wife out of their room just for one night.' He had spoken casually, now he changed the subject abruptly, as they got

44

up to go.

'It was nice of you not to mind about going straight back to Holland. We'll go away for a holiday as soon as I can get everything sorted out at the Grotehof.'

She nodded. 'Oh, the hospital, yes. Have you many private patients too?'

He sent the car tearing past a lorry. 'Yes, and shall have many more, I think. I'm looking forward to meeting your family.'

She stirred in her seat. 'Father is a little absent-minded; he doesn't live in the present when he's busy on a book, and Mother—Mother's a darling. Neither of them notices much what's going on around them, but Mother never questions anything I do. Then there's Mike—and Helen, of course, and John and Billy, they're fourteen and sixteen, and Maureen who's eleven. There are great gaps between us, but it's never seemed to matter.'

They were almost at Salisbury when she ventured to remark: 'I don't know anything about your family and I'm terrified of meeting them.'

He slowed the car down and stopped on the grass verge and turned to look at her. 'My dear Deborah—you, terrified? Why? My mother is like any other mother, perhaps a little older than yours; she must be, let me see, almost sixty. My two brothers, Pieter and Willem, are younger than I, my sister Lia comes between us—she's married to an architect and they live near Hilversum. Pieter is a pathologist in Utrecht, Willem is a lawyer—he lives in den Haag.'

'And your mother, does she live with you?'

'No, she didn't wish to go on living in the house

after my father died—I'm not sure of the reason. She has a flat close by. We see each other often.'

'So you live alone?'

'There is Wim, who sees to everything—I suppose you would call him a houseman, but he's more than that; he's been with us for so long, and there is Marijke who cooks and keeps house and Mevrouw Smit who comes in to clean. Mother took Leen, who has been with us ever since I can remember, with her when she moved to the flat.'

'Is your house large?'

'Large?' he considered her question. 'No—but it is old and full of passages and small staircases; delightful to live in but the very devil to keep clean.' He gave her a quick, sidelong glance. 'Marijke and Mevrouw Smit see to that, of course. You will be busy enough in other ways.'

'What other ways?' asked Deborah with vague suspicion.

'I told you, did I not, that I need to entertain quite a lot—oh, not riotous parties night after night, but various colleagues who come to the hospital for one reason or the other—sometimes they bring their wives, sometimes they come on their own. And there is the occasional dinner party, and we shall be asked out ourselves.'

'Oh. How did you manage before?'

He shrugged. 'Marijke coped with the odd visitor well enough, my mother acted as hostess from time to time. Remember I have been away for two years; I spent only a short time in Amsterdam each month or so, but now I am going back to live I shall be expected to do my share of entertaining. You will be of the greatest help to me if you will deal with that side of our life.'

'I'll do my best, though it's rather different from handing instruments....'

He laughed. 'Very. But if you do it half as well you will be a great success and earn my undying gratitude.'

She didn't want his gratitude; she wanted his love, but nothing seemed further from his thoughts. Dinner parties, though, would give her the opportunity to wear pretty clothes and make the most of herself—he might at least notice her as a person. She began to plan a suitable wardrobe....

The road was surprisingly empty after they had left Salisbury behind. At Warminster they turned off on to the Frome road and then, at Deborah's direction, turned off again into the byroads, through the small village of Nunney and then the still smaller one of Chantry. Her home lay a mile beyond, a Somerset farmhouse, with its back tucked cosily into the hills behind it, and beautifully restored and tended by Mr Culpeper and his wife. It looked delightful now in the afternoon sun, its windows open as was its front door, its garden a mass of colour and nothing but the open country around it. Deborah gave a small sigh of pleasure as she saw it. 'That's it,' she told Gerard.

'Charming,' he commented. 'I hope your parents will ask us back for a visit. I can see that it is a most interesting house—those windows...' he nodded towards the side of the house, 'their pediments appear most interesting.'

He brought the car to a halt before the door and as he helped her out she said with something like relief: 'Father will be delighted that you noticed them, they're very unusual. Probably he'll talk of nothing else and quite forget that we're married.'

47

They were walking to the door. 'Do you really know something of sixteenth-century building?'

'A little.' He smiled down at her and said unexpectedly: 'You look very pretty in that blue dress. Shall I ring the bell?'

For answer she shook her head and let out a piercing whistle, answered almost immediately by an equally piercing reply followed by: 'Debby, is it really you? I'm in the sitting room. Come in, darling. I can't leave this. . . .'

The hall was cool, flagstoned and bare of furniture save for an old oak chest against one wall and a grandfather clock. Deborah went through one of the open doors leading out of it and walked across the faded, still beautiful carpet to where her mother was kneeling on the floor surrounded by quantities of manuscript.

'Your father dropped the lot,' she began, preparing to get up. 'I simply have to get them into some sort of order.'

She was a great deal smaller than her daughter, but they shared the same lovely face and pansy eyes. She leaned up to hug her daughter with a happy: 'This is a lovely surprise. Are you on holiday or is it just a couple of days?' Her eyes lighted upon Gerard. 'You've had a lift—who's this?' She added thoughtfully, just as though he wasn't there: 'He's very good-looking.' She smiled at him and he returned her smile with such charm that she got to her feet, holding out a hand.

'Mother,' said Deborah with the kind of cheerful resignation her children had acquired over the years, 'this is Gerard van Doorninck. We got married this morning.'

Her parent remained blissfully calm and shook

hands. 'Well now,' she exclaimed, not in the least put out, 'isn't that nice? Debby always has known her own mind since she could handle a spoon. I should have loved to have been at the wedding, but since I wasn't we'll have a little celebration here.' She studied the tall quiet man before her. 'If I'm your mother-in-law, you're quite entitled to kiss me.'

And when he had: 'I hope Debby warned you about us. You see, my husband and I seldom go out, we're far too happy here and it's so quiet he can work undisturbed—and as for me, the days are never long enough. What do you do for a living?' she shot at him without pause.

'I'm an orthopaedic surgeon—I've been at Clare's for two years now. Deborah was my Theatre Sister.'

Mrs Culpeper nodded her slightly untidy head. 'Nasty places, operating theatres, but I suppose one can fall in love in one just as easily as anywhere else.' She spun round and addressed her daughter. 'Darling, how long are you staying, and when did you get married?'

'Just tonight, Mother, and we got married this morning.'

'In church, I hope?'

'Yes—that little one, St Joram's, just round the corner from Clare's.'

'Quite right too. Your brother's here with Helen —they're in the guest room, of course.' She handed Gerard the manuscript in an absentminded manner. 'Where am I to put you both?'

'Don't worry, Mother,' said Deborah in a hurry. 'I'll have my own room and Gerard can have Billy's —it's only for tonight—we couldn't think of turning Mike and Helen out.'

Her mother gave her a long, thoughtful look. 'Of course not, dear, and after all, you have the rest of your lives together.'

Deborah agreed with her calmly, not looking at Gerard.

'Good, that's settled—two such sensible people. Gerard, will you take these papers into the study across the hall and tell my husband that you're here? You may have to say it twice before he pays any attention; he found an interesting stone in the garden this morning—I believe it's called a shepherd's counting stone. You have a Dutch name.'

'I am Dutch, Mrs Culpeper.' And Deborah, stealing a look, was glad to see that Gerard wasn't in the least discomposed.

'I saw Queen Wilhelmina once,' Mrs Culpeper went on chattily, 'in London, during the war.' She turned to Deborah. 'Your father will be most interested, Debby. Come and put the kettle on for tea, dear.'

Deborah tucked her arm into her mother's. 'Yes, dearest, but wouldn't it be nicer if Gerard had me with him when he meets Father?'

'He looks perfectly able to introduce himself,' declared her volatile parent. 'I meant to have had tea hours ago. Come along, dear.'

Deborah looked across the room to where Gerard was standing, his arms full of papers. 'Do you mind?' she asked him.

'Not in the least. In fact it's an eminently sensible suggestion.' He smiled at her and she realized with astonishment that he was enjoying himself.

They all met again ten minutes later. She was standing at the table in the large, low-ceilinged

kitchen, cutting sandwiches and listening to her
mother's happy rambling talk while she arranged
the best Spode tea service on a tray, when the door
opened and the two men came in. Mr Culpeper
was a tall man, almost as tall as his new son-in-law,
with a thin upright body and a good-looking face
which wore its usual abstracted expression. He was
almost bald, but his moustache and neat Van Dyck
beard were still brown and thick. He came across
the room to where Deborah stood and flung an arm
around her shoulders and kissed her with fondness.
He said without preamble: 'I like your husband,
Debby—no nonsense about him, and thank God
I've at last found someone in the family who is interested in pediments.'

His eyes lighted upon the plate of sandwiches
before her and he helped himself to one and bit
into it with relish. 'Mike and Helen won't be back
just yet, so let's have tea.' He took the tray from his
wife and led the way to the sitting room.

Tea was a success, largely because Gerard joined
in the conversation with an ease of manner which
made him seem like an old friend of the family,
and later, when they had been left together in her
room—'for of course you will want to unpack for
Gerard', her mother had said—Deborah asked
him: 'You aren't bored? You see, we all love them
very much and we don't in the least mind when
they forget things and or start talking as though we
weren't there....'

He took her hands in his. 'No, Deborah, I'm not
bored, nor would I ever be here with your parents.
They are charming people and they have found the
secret of being happy, haven't they? I envy someone like your mother, who can cast down her tea-

cup and dash into the garden because a thrush is singing particularly sweetly—and your father . . . they are a devoted couple, I believe.'

She was very conscious of his hands. 'Yes, they are. I suppose that's why they view the world with such kindness and tolerance and at the same time when they want to, the two of them just retire into a—a sort of shell together—they're very unworldly.' She looked at him a little anxiously. 'I'm not a bit like them,' she assured him. 'We're all very practical and sensible; we've looked after them all our lives.' She smiled. 'Even little Maureen!'

He bent his head to kiss her cheek gently. 'That's why you're such a nice person, I expect. You know, I had forgotten that people could live like this. Perhaps the rest of us have our values wrong, working too hard, making money we have to worry about, going on holidays we don't enjoy—just because everyone else does.'

'But you're not like that.' She was quite certain of it.

'Thank you for saying that. I hope I'm not, but I'm often discontented with my life, though perhaps now that I have you for a companion I shall find more pleasure in it.'

She was breathless, but it would never do to let him see that. She moved her hands ever so slightly and he let them go at once. She turned away, saying lightly: 'I shall do my best, only you must tell me what you like and what you don't like—but you must never think that I shall be bored or find life dull. There's always so much to see and do and I love walking and staring round at things.'

He laughed. 'How restful that sounds—I like that too. We'll walk and stare as often as we can spare the time. I have a small house in Friesland and several good friends living nearby. We must spend some weekends there.'

Deborah turned to face him again, once more quite composed. 'Another house? Gerard, I've never asked you because there hasn't been much time to talk and it didn't seem important, but now I want to know. You haven't a lot of money or anything like that, have you?'

The corners of his mouth twitched, 'As to that, Deborah, I must plead guilty, for I do have a good deal of money and I own a fair amount of land besides.' He studied her face. 'Would you have married me if you had known?'

'I don't know. Yes, I do—I should have married you just the same because you would have known that I wasn't doing it for your money—at least, I hope you would.'

She saw the bleak look erase all expression from his face and wondered what she had said to cause it. 'Oh dear, have I annoyed you?'

The look had gone; perhaps she had imagined it. 'No, Deborah, and I'm glad to hear that is how you feel about it. Now supposing I take my case to Billy's room and unpack what I need, and then do you suppose we might have a stroll in your father's delightful garden?'

A suggestion to which she agreed happily enough.

It was good to see Mike and Helen again, and even if they were surprised at her news, it was only to be expected. The evening was passed pleasantly, with some of Mr Culpeper's prized Madeira brought out to drink the bride's health and a buzz of family talk interrupted by excited telephone conversations with Maureen and her brothers. And as for Deborah, the evening had become a happy dream because when they had walked in the garden, Gerard had given her a ring with the matter-of-fact observation that she should have had it before they were married; he had gone to Holland to fetch it and had forgotten to give it to her. It was a beautiful ring, a diamond, an enormous one, in a strange old-fashioned setting of two pairs of hands supporting the stone on either side. She had exclaimed over its beauty, watching its rainbow colours as she turned her hand from side to side in order to see it better, thanking him nicely, trying to forget that he himself had forgotten.

He told her that it was the traditional betrothal ring of his family. 'At least,' he had explained, 'there are two, exactly alike. My grandmother left this one to me as I was the eldest grandson, and——' he became silent and she, anxious to help him out, said: 'What a sensible idea! The other ring will be left to—to whoever is your heir—that means,' she hurried on, 'that the wives don't have to give up their engagement rings. I wonder how that all started?'

He replied casually. 'Oh, an ancestor of mine—he had a very youthful wife, and when their son married she was still a young woman and flatly refused to give up her ring, so because he loved her to distraction he had another made just like it.'

They had laughed about it together, although secretly she thought it a charming story, and later the ring had been admired and discussed and admired again. Only when she was at last in her own room lying in her white-painted bed amidst her small, familiar possessions, did she allow herself to

54

shed a few tears because the dream would never come true, of course; she would have to be sensible and make Gerard a good wife and be thankful that he at least liked her. But at the same time, she promised herself fiercely through her tears, she would never give up trying to make him love her.

She wakened early by reason of the early morning sun shining in through the open window and was on the point of getting up when there was a tap on the door and Gerard came in. His good morning was friendly, his manner as matter-of-fact as it had been the previous evening.

'I hoped you would be awake,' he said. 'I have been wondering if you would like to pay lightning visits to your brothers and sister before we leave for Holland? The boys are at Wells, aren't they? Twelve miles, no further, and Wells to Sherborne is under twenty-five and on our way, in any case, for we can pick up the Winchester road from there. The ferry doesn't sail until midnight, so as long as we don't linger over meals, we should have ample time.' He sat down on the end of her bed. 'Would you like that?'

Deborah smiled her pleasure. 'Oh, Gerard, how kind of you to think of it! I'd simply love it— you're sure there's time?'

'Positive.' He looked at his watch. 'It's half past six—a little early perhaps...?'

'Mother always gets up at seven. I'll go down and make the tea and tell her. We can have breakfast when we want, no one will mind. When do you want to leave?'

'Half past eight. I'll come down with you—better still,' he got off the bed, 'I'll go down and put the kettle on.'

By the time Deborah reached the kitchen he had the kettle boiling and a tray laid with cups and saucers and milk and sugar, which surprised her very much, for she hadn't supposed him to be the kind of man who would be handy about the house, indeed, even now, in need of a shave and in a dressing gown of great magnificence, he contrived to look more than elegant and the making of early morning tea seemed alien to his nature. There was, she guessed, a great deal to his character of which she knew nothing.

She took the tea upstairs, whispered their plans to her mother, who thought it a splendid idea and accepted them without demur, and then went back to the kitchen to drink her tea with Gerard, and because the morning was such a beautiful one, they wandered through the back door and strolled round the garden admiring the flowers, their tea cups in their hands, stopping to take an occasional sip.

'What a delightful way in which to start the day,' commented Gerard, back in the kitchen.

Deborah agreed. 'And one can do it almost anywhere,' she pointed out, 'provided there's a strip of grass and a few flowers, or a pleasant walk nearby ... have you a dog?'

'Yes, though he hasn't seen a great deal of me lately; Wim stands proxy for me, though. And there are two cats, but they belong to Marijke.'

'What do you call your dog?'

'Smith, he's a Jack Russell. He goes everywhere with me when I'm home.'

'I hope he'll like me; I could take him for walks.'

'You shall.' He took her cup from her and put it tidily in the sink. 'Shall we get dressed? What do we do about breakfast? Shall we get our own?'

'Everyone will be down—but we can always start if they're not.'

They left exactly on time amidst a chorus of good wishes and goodbyes and urgings to return as soon as possible, coupled with a great many messages from Mrs Culpeper for the boys and Maureen.

All of which Deborah faithfully passed on, although her listeners were all far too excited to pay any attention to them; the boys, naturally enough, were much more interested in the car than in their sister, and she was agreeably surprised to find how well Gerard got on with them. Her notions of him were sadly out, she admitted to herself as they took a boisterous leave of Billy and John and tore down the Fosse Way towards Sherborne and Maureen. She had always thought of him as being a perfect darling, of course, because she loved him, but also a little reserved as well as being a quiet man. He was still quiet, of course, but he obviously enjoyed the boys' company and she hadn't expected that.

It was mid-morning by now and Maureen came dancing out of her class to cast herself into her elder sister's embrace. 'Debby,' she shrilled, 'how lovely—tell me all about the wedding and what did you wear...?' She stopped to smile at Gerard and then throw herself with enthusiasm at him. 'Oh, you do look nice,' she assured him. 'Just wait till I tell the girls—can I come and stay with you soon?' She plucked impatiently at his arm. 'You're very good-looking, aren't you? which is a good thing because Debby's quite beautiful, isn't she, and thank heavens you're so tall because now she can wear high heels if she wants to.' She didn't wait for him to answer but turned her attention to Deborah again. 'You haven't told me what you wore.'

'This dress I'm wearing—it was a very quiet wedding, darling.'

Deborah smiled at her small sister; she and the boys were all so large, but Maureen took after her mother in her smallness, although at the moment she had no looks at all, only a great deal of charm.

'Shall I come and have lunch with you?' she wanted to know.

It was Gerard who answered her. 'Sorry, Maureen. We're on our way home to Holland, but how about paying us a visit in the holidays? We'll come over and fetch you.'

She flung her arms around him. 'Oh, will you? Will you really? Promise?'

'Promise.' He bent and kissed her small elfin face and looked at Deborah. 'We must go, my dear,' and he smiled half-humorously over the child's head.

They had time and to spare when they reached Dover, for the big car had eaten up the miles and they had stopped only briefly on the way. Gerard parked the car in the queue and invited Deborah to get out.

'There's an hotel just outside the dock gates,' he told her. 'We have ample time to have dinner before we go on board.'

When they reached the hotel it was long past the time that dinner was served, but Gerard seemed to have little difficulty in persuading the waiter that just this once he might stretch a point. They dined simply, watching the harbour below from their table in the window.

Deborah was surprised to find that there was a

cabin booked for her when they got on board; the crossing was barely four hours and she wasn't in the least tired, but when she said so, Gerard merely smiled and told her that it would be a good idea if she were to get some sleep. 'It can be very noisy,' he explained. 'Even if you don't sleep, you can read— I'll get you some magazines. And my cabin is next to yours, so you have only to knock if you want anything.'

She thanked him, wishing that they could have spent the time together talking, for she suspected that once they got to his home he would be swallowed up in his work almost at once and she might see very little of him. He was going to take up the appointment which had been waiting for him in the hospital where he had been a consultant for some years; she felt sure that he would want to start at once.

She lay down on her bunk and pulled a blanket over her and opened the first of the magazines. Long before the ferry sailed, she was asleep.

CHAPTER FOUR

DEBORAH was called with a cup of tea and a polite request from the steward that she would join her husband in the lounge as soon as she was ready. Gerard was waiting for her, looking, at four-fifteen in the morning, quite immaculate, so that she was glad that she had taken trouble with her own appearance; her face nicely made up, her hair as neat as it always was, her blue outfit fresh and creaseless from its careful hanging while she slept.

It was still dark when they landed, but Gerard

shot away as though he knew the road blindfold, which, she conceded, was probably the case. But although he drove fast he didn't allow it to interfere with the casual conversation which he carried on, explaining in which direction they were going, pointing out the towns as they passed through them and warning her when they approached the frontier between Belgium and Holland.

It was growing lighter now. They passed through the small town of Sluis with its narrow, twisting streets, still so quiet in the early morning and then out again on to the straight tree-lined road, making for the ferry at Breskens. 'There is another route,' he told her, 'through Antwerp and Breda, but it's usually loaded with traffic. Even with a possible delay on the ferry I find this way shorter now that the new bridges and roads are open to Rotterdam.'

It was light enough to see by now and Deborah, wide awake, asked endless questions and could barely wait to drink the coffee he fetched for her on board the ferry, because she wanted to see everything at once as they crossed the great river. She thought Flushing disappointingly dull, although the sea-front, which she could see in the distance, was probably delightful with its long line of hotels facing the beach. But she had little enough chance to do more than glimpse it, for Gerard skirted the town and took the motorway to Goes, past factories and shipyards and a great deal of dreary flat country. She would have liked to have commented upon this, for after Somerset she found it depressing, but she held her tongue, and presently, once they were past Goes, on the fine road crossing the islands, speeding towards Rotterdam, she cheered up, for here the country was green and pretty in the morning sunlight and the houses with their steep red roofs and the solid farms looked delightful enough. Even Rotterdam, even though there was little to see but towering flats and factories and docks, was interesting and bustling with early workers, and the more so because Gerard told her a great deal about it as he eased the car through the ever-increasing traffic with a patience and good humour she was sure she would never have had.

Once through the city and on the motorway once more, Gerard remarked: 'We could have crossed the river lower down and gone through Europoort on the new road to Delft, but you have already seen so many factories and blast furnaces—this way is more interesting and we can stop in Delft and have breakfast. Reyndorp's Prinsenhof will be open by now.'

Delft, Deborah discovered at once, was quite a different kettle of fish. Gerard parked the car in one of the main streets of the picturesque little town and led her across the road to the restaurant, where they obligingly served them with an ample breakfast at a table in a window overlooking the street. There were already plenty of people going to work on their bicycles, milk carts, bread carts, carts loaded with vegetables and weaving in and out of them, hordes of schoolchildren on their motorised bikes.

'Everything seems to start very early,' Deborah exlaimed. 'Look, there's a shop open already.'

'A good many open at eight o'clock, sometimes earlier. I suppose we breakfast earlier than they do in England—we lunch at midday, and most people have an evening meal about six o'clock.'

'That makes a very long evening.'

His blue eyes twinkled. 'Ah, yes—but the Dutchman likes to sit at home reading his paper, drinking his glass of gin and surrounded by his wife and children. Perhaps you find that dull, but we don't think so.'

Deborah shook her head; it didn't sound dull at all. She enjoyed for a fleeting moment a vivid picture of Gerard and herself on either side of the hearth with a clutch of small van Doornincks between them. She brushed the dream aside briskly; he had told her that he had a great many friends and entertained quite frequently and that they would go out fairly often, and perhaps, as there were to be no little van Doornincks, that was a very good thing.

They were less than forty miles from Amsterdam now and once back on the motorway it seemed even less. They seemed to come upon the city suddenly, rising abruptly from the flat fields around it and Gerard had perforce to slow down, turning and twisting through narrow streets and along canals which looked so charming that she wished that they might stop so that she might take a better look. Presently he turned into a busy main street, only to cross it and turn down another narrow street bordering a canal.

'Where are we now?' she ventured to ask.

'The Keizersgracht. It's a canal which runs almost in a full circle round the city. There are other canals which follow its line exactly, rather like a spider's web. All of them contain beautiful old houses, most of which are embassies or warehouses or offices now.'

She peered around her; the houses were large, tall and built on noble lines with big square windows and great front doors, and despite this they contrived to look homelike. She said so and heard him laugh. 'I'm glad you like them, for here we are at my—our home.'

He had slowed the car and stopped outside a double-fronted, red brick house, its front door reached by a double row of steps, its windows, in orderly rows, large and square, its roof, Deborah could see, craning her pretty neck, ended in a rounded gable which leaned, very slightly, forward. She would have liked to have stood and stared, just as she would have paused by the canals, but Gerard was waiting for her. He took her hand as she got out of the car and drew it under his arm and mounted the steps to the door which opened as they reached it.

This would be Wim, she guessed, a short, thick-set man with grizzled hair and blue eyes set in a round, cheerful face. He shook Gerard's proffered hand with pleasure and when Gerard introduced him to Deborah, took her hand too and said in heavily accented, difficult English:

'I am happy, Mevrouw. It is a moment to rejoice. My felicitations.'

She thanked him, and without knowing it pleased him mightily by remarking on his knowledge of English, adding the rider that she hoped that her Dutch would be as good. Upon this small wave of mutual friendliness they entered the hall, while Wim closed the door behind them.

The hall was narrow, although it had two deep alcoves, each with a wall table and a mirror hanging above. Along one side, between them, was a double door, carved and arched, and beyond them a carved wooden staircase. On the other side of the hall there were three doors and an arched opening reached by several descending steps, coming up which now was a tall, thin, middle-aged woman, with pale hair which could have been flaxen or equally well grey. She wore a rather old-fashioned black dress and a large print apron and although her face seemed severe she was smiling broadly now. She broke at once into speech and then turned to Deborah, her hand held out, and began all over again. When she finally stopped Deborah smiled and nodded and asked Gerard urgently: 'Please will you tell Marijke that I'll learn Dutch just as soon as I can, so that we can have the pleasure of talking to each other?'

She watched him as he repeated what she had said in his own language. It sounded like nonsense to her, but she supposed that if she worked hard enough at it, she would at least learn the bare bones of it in a few weeks, and anyway, it seemed that she had said the right thing, for Marijke was smiling more broadly than ever. She shook Deborah's hand again, said something to Gerard in which the word coffee was easily recognisable, and went back down the steps while Wim opened the first of the doors in the hall for them to enter.

The room had a very high ceiling of ornamental plaster work and panelled walls ending in a shelf two thirds of the way up, upon which rested a collection of china which Deborah supposed was Delft. The furniture was comfortable, upholstered in a russet velvet which went well with the deep blues and greens and ambers of the vast carpet. The lampstands were delicate china figures holding aloft cream and russet shades. She found the room delightful, although it was a good deal more *splendid than she had expected.*

They had their coffee sitting side by side upon a small settee covered in exquisite needlework, and somehow the sight of the old, beautifully simple silver coffee service on its heavy tray flanked by cups which should by rights have been in some museum, so old and fragile were they, depressed her; she had expected comfort, certainly, but this was more than comfort, it was an ageless way of life which she would have to learn to live. She shivered a little, thinking of the dinner parties; possibly the guests would dislike her. . . .

'It's all strange, isn't it?' Gerard was at his most placid, 'but it's home. All this'—he waved a large, square hand—'has been handed down from one son to the next, whether we have wanted it or not, though to be honest, I love every stick and stone of the place, and I hope that you will too.' He put down his coffee cup. 'You will be tired. Would you like to go to bed?'

She was quite taken aback. 'Oh, no, thank you, I'm not in the least tired. If I might just go to my room, I could unpack and change my clothes. I expect you have a great deal to do.'

She saw at once that she had said the right thing, for the relief on his face, quickly suppressed, was real enough. 'Yes, I have. Shall we meet again for lunch? I've asked Mother round.' He smiled nicely. 'You'll feel better once you have met her.'

She got to her feet and he walked with her to the door, opened it and called for Marijke. Even as Deborah started up the staircase in the wake of the older woman, she heard him cross the hall to the front door.

Her room was at the back of the house and her

luggage was already in it. As soon as Marijke had left her she went to the window, to discover a small garden below, with a fountain in its centre and tubs of flowers grouped round it. There was grass too, only a very small circle of it, but it looked green and fresh, and brooding over the cheerful little plot was a copper beech, rustling faintly in the wind.

Deborah turned her back on the pleasant scene presently to survey the room; large and airy and furnished in the style of Chippendale, probably genuine pieces, she thought, caressing the delicate lines of the dressing table. There was a vast cupboard along one wall with a door beside it and on the opposite wall a tallboy. The bed was wide and covered with the same pastel pale chintz as the curtains, the carpet was a deep cream and the lamps and small armchair were covered in pink striped silk. A beautiful room. She sighed her content and hastened to open the first of its three doors. A bathroom with another door leading back on to the landing, she glanced quickly at its luxury and crossed the room. The second door opened on to a short corridor lined with cupboards and lighted by a window on its other side, there was a door at its end and she opened that too and went in. Gerard's luggage was there, so this was his room, smaller than her own and a little severe but just as comfortable. It, too, had a door leading on to the landing and a bathroom built into a deep alcove.

She went back the way she had come and had a bath and put on a plain cotton jersey dress the colour of apricots, then sat down at the dressing table and did her face with great care and arranged her hair in its smooth wings with the chignon at the back, put her engagement ring back on her finger and, after a long look at herself in the handsome mirror, made her way downstairs.

There were voices in the sitting room and she heard Gerard's laugh. His mother had arrived. She trod firmly down the staircase and had almost reached the bottom when he appeared in the sitting room doorway.

'I thought I heard you,' he greeted her smilingly, and whistled briefly. A small dog scampered past him and across the hall. 'Here's Smith, I've just fetched him from the vet.'

Smith had halted in front of her and she sat down on the stairs and put out a gentle hand. 'Hullo, Smith,' she said, 'I hope we're going to be friends.' The dog stared at her with bright black eyes, and after a moment wagged his tail and allowed her to stroke him, and when she got to her feet, walked quite soberly beside her to where Gerard was waiting.

He took her arm as they went into the sitting room and led her over to the window where his mother sat. She wasn't at all what Deborah had imagined she would be; small for a start, almost as small as her own mother, and her eyes were brown and kind. Her nose was an autocratic little beak, but the mouth below it was as kind as the eyes. She stood up as they reached her and said in excellent English:

'Deborah, my dear, welcome to the family. You do not know how happy I am to see Gerard married, and to such a lovely girl. I must say that he described you very well, but I have been longing to meet you. Gerard, bring a chair over here so that I can talk to Deborah—and pour us all a drink.'

And when Deborah was seated and he had gone to the other end of the room where the drinks were laid out on a Pembroke table: 'You must not think that I order him about, my dear. Indeed, I would not dream of doing any such thing, but just now and again I pretend to do so and he pretends to do as I wish. It works very well for us both. And now tell me, what do you think of this house?'

'I've only seen a very little of it; Gerard had things to do.... What I have seen I find quite beautiful.'

The older lady nodded complacently. 'I knew you would like it—love it, I hope. I did, still do, but my husband and I were devoted and without him it doesn't seem the same—besides, I was determined to leave it the moment Gerard told me about you.' She smiled faintly. 'I think I guessed before that.' She gave Deborah a long, thoughtful look and Deborah looked back at her, her eyes quiet.

'Then he lived in a huge flat,' his mother explained, taking it for granted that Deborah knew what she was talking about. She shuddered delicately. 'He loathed it, although he never said so....' she broke off as Gerard came towards them.

'Champagne,' he announced, 'as befits an occasion,' and he lifted his glass to Deborah.

They lunched without haste, although the moment they had finished Gerard excused himself on the pretext of a visit to the hospital as well as his consulting rooms to see what his secretary had got for him. 'Mother will love to show you the house,' he told Deborah as he prepared to leave. 'Don't wait tea—I don't expect to be back much before six.'

She smiled and nodded because that was what

she would have to learn to do cheerfully from now on; watch him go through the front door and then wonder where he had gone to and what he was doing and who he was with ... it didn't bear thinking about. She turned to her mother-in-law with a too-bright smile and professed herself eager to explore the house.

Gerard had been right when he had described it as being full of narrow passages and old staircases, and some of the rooms were very small, although all were charmingly furnished. Deborah wandered up and down with Mevrouw van Doorninck, stopping to peer at family portraits or admire a mirror or one of the trifles of silver or china with which the house was filled. When they had finally completed their tour, she said: 'I feel as though I had turned you out, Mevrouw van Doorninck. How could you bear to leave?'

'It was a wrench, Deborah, but I have some of the furniture in the flat and all my personal treasures. I had made up my mind before Gerard's father died that I would leave, although Gerard didn't want it. You see, I wanted him to marry again, and if I had stayed here, he might never have done so. But living on his own, without a wife to greet his guests and arrange his dinner parties and run the house ... that sounds all wrong, my dear, but I don't mean it to be. He talked about you several times when he came home from Clare's, you know. He told me what a quiet, sensible girl you were and how capable and charming, and I hoped that he would ask you to marry him, and you see that I have my wish.' She patted Deborah's hand. 'You must come and see me very soon—tomorrow if Gerard can spare the time, and then in a day or so I shall give a small dinner party for you so that you can meet the family. You will feel a little strange at first, but I'm sure that Gerard will arrange for you to have Dutch lessons and show you round Amsterdam and show you off to his friends. Very soon you will settle down quite nicely.'

And indeed, to all intents and purposes Deborah did settle down. To the world around her she presented a calm, unruffled face, charming manners and a smiling acceptance of her new way of life. True to her promise, Mevrouw van Doorninck had given her dinner party, where she had met Gerard's sister and brothers; three nice people anxious to make her feel at home. They were considerably younger than he and she liked them at once. She met the children too; Lia had two boys, and Pieter and Willem had a boy and a girl each, all rather alike with pale flaxen hair and blue eyes and just as willing as their parents to absorb her into the family, the older ones trying out their school English on her, the toddlers not caring what language she spoke.

And because Gerard had done nothing about it, she had asked Wim's advice and found herself an old dry-as-dust professor, long retired from his university chair at Leiden, and applied herself assiduously to her Dutch—a disheartening task, she soon discovered, what with the verbs coming at the end of a sentence instead of the middle and the terrible grammar, but at least she had learned a few dozen words, correctly pronounced—the old professor had seen to that. It was amazing the amount one could learn when one applied oneself and one had, sadly enough, time idle on one's hands.

But there was one person amongst the many

whom she met whom she could not like—Claude van Trapp, a man younger than Gerard and a friend of the family since their boyhood days. He was good-looking, and what she would suppose could be described as good fun. He was certainly an intelligent man, and yet Deborah mistrusted him; she found his charm false, and the snide remarks he let fall from time to time seemed to her to be spiteful more than witty. It surprised her that Gerard tolerated him with a careless good humour which annoyed her, and when the opportunity occurred she had, in a roundabout way, tried to discover the reason for this. But he had only laughed and shrugged his great shoulders. 'A little sharp in the tongue, perhaps,' he conceded, 'but we have known each other since our pram days, you know.'

She hadn't pursued the subject, for it was apparent that Gerard was so tolerant of Claude's comings and goings to the house that he hardly noticed him and indeed probably believed him to be the boy he had known. She knew him to be incapable of pettiness or meanness himself, so he certainly wouldn't expect it or look for it in his friends. He was, in fact, blinded by familiarity and she could do nothing about it. But after the first few meetings, she contrived to slip away on some pretext or other when Claude came to the house; easily enough done, for she was taking her duties seriously and there was always something to do around the house, and when his company was unavoidable she behaved with an impeccable politeness towards him, meeting his malicious titbits of gossip and innuendoes with a charming vagueness, ignoring his thinly veiled contempt for her apparent dimness, just as she ignored his admiring glances and sly looks.

It was after she had been in Holland a bare three weeks that Claude called one afternoon. She was in the little garden with Smith, sitting under the shade of the copper beech while she learned the lesson Professor de Wit had set her. It was a beautiful day and she felt a little drowsy, for the night before they had given their first dinner party, quite a small one but nerve-racking. All the same, it had been a success and she had been elated by Gerard's pleased comments afterwards; she had even allowed herself the satisfaction of knowing that he had admired her in the new dress she had bought for the occasion, a pale green silk sheath. She had worn the thick gold chain his mother had given her and of course, her lovely ring. After the guests had gone home, he had followed her into the drawing room and leaned against the wall, watching her as she went round plumping up cushions, restoring chairs to their original places and moving the small tables carefully. It was a room she already loved, its grandeur mitigated by a pleasant homeliness, brought about, she was sure, by the fact that it was lived in. She moved a priceless Rockingham vase to a place of safety and said with satisfaction: 'There, now it looks like itself again—I think your friends must love coming here, Gerard.'

'I daresay.' He sauntered across the pale Aubusson carpet towards her. 'A pleasant and successful evening, Deborah, and you were a perfect hostess. I knew that you would make me an excellent wife— you are also a very charming and beautiful one.' He bent and kissed her. 'Thank you, my dear.'

She had waited, hoping foolishly that he might

72

say more; that he found her attractive, even that he was falling a little in love with her, but his bland: 'What a wise choice I have made,' gave her little consolation. She had said a little woodenly that she was pleased that she was living up to his good opinion of her and wished him a good night, to go to her room and lie very wide awake in her vast bed until the early hours of the morning. Three weeks, she had reminded herself, and that was only a fraction of the lifetime ahead of her, playing the hostess to Gerard's friends, helping him in every way she could, keeping his home just as he wanted it, taking an interest in his work on those all too rare occasions when he talked about it.

She remembered that she didn't even know where the hospital was, nor for that matter, his consulting rooms, and when she had asked him he had said kindly that he imagined she had enough to fill her days without bothering her head about such things, and then, sensing her hurt, had offered to take her to the hospital and show her round.

It was almost as though he were keeping her at arms' length ... and yet he had been good to her and very kind; she had a more than generous allowance, and true to his promise, Maureen was to visit them in a week's time and when Deborah had admired a crocodile handbag he had bought it for her without hesitation. He had bought her a car too—a Fiat 500—and opened accounts at all the larger shops for her. He was generous to a fault, and she repaid him in the only ways she knew how; by breakfasting with him each morning even though he was immersed in his post which she opened for him, and after he had gone, sorted for his secretary to attend to when she came during the morning. And she was always waiting for him when he got home in the evenings, sitting with Smith in the garden or reading in the sitting room. She wasn't sure if this was what he wanted her to do, and it was difficult to tell because he was unfailingly courteous to her, but at least she was there if he should want to talk. In a week or two, when she knew him a little better, she would ask him.

She applied herself to her Dutch grammar again and twiddled Smith's ears gently. There was still an hour before Wim would bring the tea and Gerard had said that he would be late that evening. She sighed and began to worry her way through the past tense of the verb *to be*.

Her earnest efforts were interrupted by the appearance of Claude. She looked up in some surprise as he lounged across the little plot of grass.

'Oh, hullo, Claude,' she forced her voice to politeness. 'I didn't hear the bell.'

'I walked in,' he told her coolly. 'A lovely afternoon and nothing to do—I thought I might invite myself to tea.'

She closed her book. 'Why, of course,' and felt irritated when he sat down beside her and took it from her.

'What's this? Dutch grammar—my goodness, you are trying hard, aren't you? Does Gerard know, or did he fix it up for you?'

She became evasive. 'I have lessons from a dear old professor—it's a difficult language, but I know quite a few words already, as well as one or two sentences.'

'"I love you," for instance, or should it be "do you love me?", he asked, and added: 'Oh, I've annoyed you—I must apologise, but the idea of Gerard loving anyone is so amusing that I can't help wondering.'

Deborah turned to look at him, amazed at the fury of the rage she was bottling up. 'I know that you are a very old friend of Gerard's, but I don't care to discuss him with anyone. I hope you understand that.'

'Lord, yes,' he said easily. 'You have my fullest admiration, Debby—it must be hellishly difficult.'

'I prefer you not to call me Debby,' she told him austerely, and then, her curiosity getting the better of her good sense: 'What must be difficult?'

He grinned. 'Why, to be married to Gerard, of course. Everyone knows what a mess he made of his first marriage—no wonder the poor girl died. . . .'

She had had enough; if he had intended to anger her, he had succeeded; her fury bubbled over as she got up, restraining herself with difficulty from slapping his smiling face. She said in a voice which shook with anger: 'I was told you were Gerard's friend, but you aren't behaving like a friend! I haven't the least idea what you're talking about, and I don't want to know. I think you should go—now!'

He didn't budge, but sat looking up at her, grinning still. 'If only I knew you better there would be a number of interesting questions I should like to ask, though I daresay you wouldn't answer them. I had no idea that you had such a nasty temper. Does Gerard know about it, I wonder?'

'Does Gerard know what?' asked Gerard from the shadow of the door, and Deborah jumped at the sound of his quiet voice, hating herself for doing it, whereas Claude didn't move, merely said: 'Hullo, there— early home, aren't you? The newly married man and all that?'

Deborah suddenly didn't care if Claude was an old family friend or not; she said hotly: 'I was just asking Claude to leave the house, but now you're here, Gerard, I think he should tell you why.'

'No need, my dear.' Gerard sounded almost placid. 'I'm afraid I have been guilty of eavesdropping—it was such an interesting conversation and I couldn't bring myself to break it up.'

He strolled across the grass to join them. 'Get up,' he ordered Claude, and his voice was no longer placid, but cold and contemptuous. 'It is a strange thing,' he commented to no one in particular, 'how blind one becomes to one's friends, though perhaps friends isn't quite the operative word. Deborah is quite right, I think you should leave my house— this instant, Claude, and not come back.'

Claude had got to his feet. 'You're joking....'

'No.'

'Just because I was going to tell Debby....' he turned to look at her, 'Deborah—about Sasja? Don't be ridiculous, Gerard, if I don't tell her someone else will.'

'Possibly, but they would tell the truth. What were you going to tell her, Claude?' The coldness of his voice was tinged with interest.

'I——? Only that....'

Deborah had had enough; she interrupted sharply: 'I'm going to my room.'

Her husband put out a hand and took her arm in a gentle grip which kept her just where she was, but he didn't look at her.

'Get out,' he advised Claude softly, 'get out before I remember that you were once a friend of mine, and if you come here again, annoying my wife, I'll make mincemeat of you.'

Deborah watched Claude go, taking no notice of his derisive goodbye. She didn't look at Gerard either, only after the faint slam of the front door signalled the last of Claude van Trapp did she say once more: 'If you don't mind—I've a headache.... I'll get Wim to bring you out some tea.'

'Wait, Deborah.' Gerard had turned her round to face him, his hands on her shoulders. 'I'm sorry about this—I had no idea that Claude ... thank you for being loyal, and in such circumstances. You have every right to be angry, for I should have told you the whole sorry story before our marriage, but it is one I have tried to forget over the years, and very nearly succeeded—the idea of digging it all up again....'

'Then I don't want to hear it,' declared Deborah. 'What possible difference could it make anyway? It isn't as though we're—we're....'

'In love?' he finished for her. 'No, but we are friends, companions if you like, sharing our lives, and you have the right to know—and I should like to tell you.' He had pulled her close and his arms were very comforting—but that was all they were. She leaned her head against his shoulder and said steadily: 'I'm listening.'

'I married Sasja when I was twenty-eight. She was nineteen and gay and pretty and so young. I was studying for my fellowship and determined to be a success because I loved—still love—my work and nothing less than success would do. It was my fault, I suppose, working night after night when we should have been out dancing, or going to parties or the theatre. Perhaps I loved her, but it wasn't the right kind of love, and I couldn't understand why she hadn't the patience to wait until I had got my feet on the bottom rung of the ladder, just as she couldn't understand why I should choose to spend hour after hour working when I could have been taking her out.' He sighed. 'You see, I had thought that she would be content looking after our home—we had a modern flat in Amsterdam—and having our children.' His even voice became tinged with bitterness. 'She didn't want or like children and she had no interest in my work. After a year she found someone else and I, God forgive me, didn't discover it until she was killed, with the other man, in a plane crash.'

Deborah said into the superfine cloth of his shoulder: 'I'm sorry, Gerard, but I'm glad I know.' She lifted her face to meet his. 'I wanted to slap Claude—I wish I had!'

She was rewarded by his faint smile. 'He was right in a way, you know—I was really responsible for Sasja's death.'

'He was not! He made it sound underhand and beastly—quite horrible—and it wasn't like that, nor was it your fault.'

'Yes, it was, Deborah—I married the wrong girl just because I was, for a very short time, in love with her. Now you know why I don't want to become involved again—why I married you.'

'And if that's a compliment, it's a mighty odd one,' she told herself silently, and swallowed back the tears tearing at her throat.

Out loud, she said matter-of-factly: 'Well, now you've told me, we won't talk about Sasja again.' She took a heartening breath. 'You don't still love her?'

His voice was nicely reassuring. 'Quite sure. My

love wore thin after a very few months—when she died I had none left.'

And Deborah's heart gave a guilty skip of joy; she was sorry about Sasja, but it was a long time ago, and she hadn't treated Gerard very well. She registered a mental resolve to find out more about her from her mother-in-law when the occasion was right, for it seemed to her that Gerard was very likely taking a blame which wasn't his. She drew away from him and said briskly: 'I'll get the tea, shall I? Would you like it out here?'

She was glad of the few minutes' respite to compose herself once more into the quiet companion he expected when he came home; she and Wim took the tea out between them and when she sat down again under the copper beech she saw that Gerard was leafing through her Dutch grammar.

She poured the tea and waited for him to speak. 'Something I forgot,' he said slowly. 'I should have arranged lessons for you.'

'As a matter of fact,' she began carefully, sugaring his tea and handing him the cup, 'I do have lessons. I asked around and I go to a dear old man called Professor de Wit four times a week. He's very good and fearfully stern. I've had eight lessons so far. He gives me a great deal of homework.'

Gerard put the book down. 'I have underestimated you, Deborah,' he observed wryly. 'Tell me, why are you going to all this trouble?'

She was taken aback. 'Trouble? It's no trouble, it's something to do. Besides, how can I be a good wife if I can't even understand my husband's language? Not all your friends speak English.'

He was staring at her, frowning a little. 'You regard our marriage as a job to be done well—is that

79

how you think of it, Deborah?'

She took a sandwich with a hand which trembled very slightly; it would never do for him to get even an inkling. 'Yes,' she declared brightly. 'Isn't that what you wanted?' and when he didn't reply, went on: 'Maureen will be here next week. I know you won't have any time to spare, but will you suggest the best outings for her? I thought I'd take her to Volendam in the Fiat—all those costumes, you know—and then we can go to the Rijksmuseum and the shops and go round the canals in one of those boats. I'm longing to go—and the Palace, if it's open.'

'My poor Deborah, I've neglected you.'

'No. I knew that you were going to be busy, you told me so. Besides, I've had several weeks in which to find my own feet.'

He smiled. 'You're as efficient a wife and hostess as you were a Theatre Sister,' he told her. And because she thought he expected it of her, she laughed gaily and assured him that that had been her ambition.

Presently he got to his feet. 'I've a couple of patients to see at my consulting rooms,' he told her, 'but I'll be back within the hour. Are we doing anything this evening?'

She shook her head. Perhaps he would take her out—she would wear the new dress. . . .

'Good. Could we dine a little earlier? I've a mass of work to do; a couple of quiet hours in the study would be a godsend to me.'

Deborah even managed a smile. 'Of course—half past six? That will give you a lovely long evening.'

He hesitated. 'And you?'

80

She gave him a calm smiling look from her lovely eyes. 'I've simply masses of letters to write,' she lied.

CHAPTER FIVE

THEY fetched Maureen the following week, travelling overnight to arrive at Sherborne in the early morning, picking up an ecstatic child beside herself with excitement, and driving on to Deborah's home for lunch. The boys were home for the half-term holiday too and it was a noisy hilarious meal, with the whole family talking at once, although Mr Culpeper confined his conversation to Gerard, because, as he remarked a little severely to the rest of his family, he appeared to be the only calm person present. He had, it was true, greeted his various children with pleasure, but as he had just finished translating an Anglo-Saxon document of some rarity, and wished to discuss it with someone intelligent, he took little part in the rather excited talk. Deborah could hear various snatches of her learned parent's rambling dissertation from time to time and wondered if Gerard was enjoying it as much as he appeared to be. She decided that he was; he was even holding his own with her father, something not many people were able to do. They exchanged brief smiles and she turned back to Maureen's endless questions.

They left shortly afterwards, driving fast to catch the night ferry, and Maureen, who had sat in front with Gerard, had to be persuaded to go to the cabin with Deborah when they got on board; the idea of staying up all night, and on a boat, was an alluring one, only the pleasures in store in the morning, dangled before her sleepy eyes by Gerard, convinced her that a few hours of sleep was a small price to pay for the novelty of driving through a foreign country at half past four in the morning.

The weather was fine, although it was still dark when they landed. Maureen, refreshed by a splendid nap, sat beside Gerard once more, talking without pause. Deborah wondered if he minded, although it was hard to tell from his manner, which was one of amused tolerance towards his small sister-in-law. Once or twice he turned to speak to her and she thought that there was more warmth in his voice when he spoke, but that could be wishful thinking, for after the unpleasant business with Claude and all that he had told her about his marriage to Sasja, she had hoped that perhaps his feelings might have deepened from friendship to even the mildest of affection.

She was to think that on several occasions during the next few days, but never with certainty. Gerard, it seemed, could spare the time to take his small relative round and about where he had not found it possible with herself, and Deborah caught herself wondering if he was seizing the opportunity to get upon a closer footing with herself. He drove them to Volendam, obligingly helped Maureen purchase postcards and souvenirs, admired the costumed villagers, standing ready to have their photos taken by the tourists, and when Maureen wished that she had a camera so that she could take her own pictures, purchased one for her. And what was more, he showed nothing but pleasure when she flung her arms around him and thanked him extravagantly for it.

They lunched that day at Wieringerwerf, after the briefest of visits to Hoorn. The restaurant was on the main road, a large, bustling place, colourful with flags and brightly painted chairs and tables on its terraces; not at all the sort of place Gerard would choose to go to for himself, Deborah suspected, but Maureen, eyeing the coloured umbrellas and the comfortable restaurant, pronounced it super. She chose her lunch from an enormous menu card and told Gerard that he was super too, and when he laughed, said:

'But it's true, you are super. I'm not surprised that Debby married you. If you could have waited a year or two, I'd have married you myself. Perhaps you have some younger brothers?'

'Married, I'm afraid, my dear—but I have a number of cousins. I'll arrange for you to meet them next time you come and you can look them over.' Deborah saw no mockery in his face and loved him for it.

Maureen agreed to this. 'Though I don't suppose you'll want me again for a little while. I mean, there are so many of us, aren't there? You'll only want a few at a time.'

Gerard glanced at Deborah. 'Oh, I don't know,' he said easily. 'I think it would be rather fun if all of you were to come over and spend Christmas. There's plenty of room.'

She beamed at him. 'I say, you really are the greatest! I'll tell Mother, so's she can remind Father about it, then it won't come as a surprise to him—he forgets, you know.'

She polished off an enormous icecream embellished with whipped cream, chocolate, nuts and fruit, and sighed blissfully. 'Where do we go next?' she wanted to know.

Gerard glanced at his watch. 'I'm afraid back home. I have a list this afternoon at four o'clock.'

'You won't be home for dinner?' asked Deborah, trying to sound casual.

'I very much doubt it. Can you amuse yourselves?'

'Of course.' Had she not been amusing herself times without number all these weeks? 'Shall I get you something cooked when you come in?'

'Would you? It could be any time.'

It was late when he got back, Marijke had gone to bed, leaving Wim to lay a tray for his master. So it was Deborah who went down to the kitchen and heated soup and made an omelette and a fresh fruit salad and carried them up to the dining room.

She arranged everything on the table and when Gerard was seated went to sit herself in one of the great armchairs against the wall.

'I hope it was successful,' she essayed, not knowing if he was too tired to talk or if he wanted to talk about it.

He spooned his soup. 'Entirely successful. You're referring to the case this afternoon—I had no idea that you knew about it.'

'I didn't. You always have a list on Thursday afternoons, but you have never been later than eight o'clock, so I guessed....'

He laughed. 'I keep forgetting that you've worked for me for two years. It was an important patient and he had come a long way in the hope that I could help him, but he refused utterly to allow me to begin the operation until his wife had arrived.'

'Was it a chondroma?'

'Yes.'

'Poor man, but I'm glad you could help him. His wife must be so thankful.'

Gerard began on the omelette. 'I imagine so,' and when he didn't say anything else she said presently: 'Thank you for spending so much time with us today. Maureen loved it.'

'And you?'

'I loved it too; it's all foreign to me, even though I live here now.'

He frowned. 'I keep forgetting that too. I shan't have a minute to spare tomorrow, but I'll manage an afternoon the day after—have you any plans?'

'Could we go somewhere for tea? Maureen loves going out to tea, especially if it's combined with sightseeing. I could take her on a round of the canals tomorrow.'

He speared the last of the omelette, complimented her upon her cooking and observed: 'I know I'm booked up for tomorrow, but how would it be if you both came to the hospital and had a look round? I'll get one of the housemen to take you round. Go to the—no, better still, I'll come home and pick you up, only you mustn't keep me waiting. Paul van Goor can look after you and see you into a taxi afterwards. Would you like that?'

She said very quietly: 'Enormously,' wondering if he was being kind to Maureen or if he was allowing her to share his life just a little at last. 'If you'll tell us what time you want us to be ready, we'll be waiting.' She got up. 'Would you like the brandy? I'm going to fetch the coffee.'

'Shall we go into the sitting room and share the pot between us?'

She loathed coffee so late at night, but she would gladly swallow pints of it if he wanted her to talk to. Perhaps the operation had been a bit of a strain —she had no idea who the important patient might be and she had too much sense to ask. All the same, when she had poured coffee for them both she asked him: 'I'd love to hear about the op if it wouldn't bore you—which method did you use?'

She had done the right thing, she could sense that. He told her, using terms he had no need to explain, describing techniques she understood and could comment upon with intelligence. It was very late when he had finished, and when he apologised for keeping her up she waved a careless hand and said in a carefully matter-of-fact voice: 'I enjoyed it.'

She took the tray back to the kitchen, wished him goodnight and went quickly upstairs, because she couldn't trust herself to preserve her careful, tranquil manner any longer.

She and Maureen were to be ready at half past one on the following afternoon, and at exactly that time Gerard came for them. He was preoccupied but, as always, courteous during the short drive. The Grotehof hospital was in the centre of the city, tucked away behind some of its oldest houses. The building was old too, but had been extended and modernized until it was difficult to see where the old ended and the new began. The entrance was in the old part, through a large, important door leading to a vast tiled hall. It was here that Gerard, with a muttered word of apology, handed them over with a hasty word of introduction to a young and cheerful houseman, Paul van Goor, who, obviously primed as to his task, led them through a labyrinth of corridors to the children's ward, talking all the time in excellent English.

From there they went to the surgical block, the medical block, the recreation rooms, the Accident Room, the dining room for the staff and lastly the theatre block, the newest addition to the hospital, he told them proudly. It consisted of six theatres, two for general surgery, one for E.N.T., one for cardio-thoracic work and two for orthopaedics. They couldn't go inside, of course, although Deborah longed to do so, and when she peered through the round window in the swing doors she felt a pang of regret that it was no longer her world; she amended that—the regret was because it was still Gerard's world and she no longer had a share in it, for at least at Clare's she worked with him. Now she was a figurehead in his house, running it smoothly and efficiently, dressing to do him credit, living with him and yet not sharing his life.

She sighed, and Paul asked her if she was tired and when she said no, suggested that they might like to go back through the hospital garden, very small but lovingly tended. They returned via lengthy staircases and roundabout passages, Deborah deep in thought, Maureen and Paul talking earnestly. They were passing a great arched doorway when a nurse flung it open and coming towards them from the other side was Gerard, a different Gerard, surrounded by a group of housemen and students, his registrar, the Ward Sister and a handful of nurses. If he saw them he took no notice; Deborah hadn't expected him too. She managed to snatch at Maureen's hand as she lifted it to wave to him.

'No, you can't, darling,' she said urgently. 'Not here, it wouldn't do. I'll explain later.'

She had done her best to do so on their way to Mevrouw van Doorninck's flat in the taxi Paul had got for them, but all Maureen said was: 'Oh, Debby, how stuffy you are—he's my brother-in-law, and you're married to him, of course he can wave to us if he wants to; important people do just what they like and no one minds.'

She was inclined to argue about it; fortunately she was kept too occupied for the rest of the afternoon, for Gerard's mother had gathered the family together to meet Maureen and the party was a merry one. 'Only,' as Mevrouw van Doorninck declared to Deborah, as they drank their tea and nibbled the thin sugary biscuits, 'it's such a pity that Gerard can't be here too. I had hoped now that he was married ... it is as though he is afraid to be happy again.' She glanced at Deborah, who said nothing at all, and went on presently: 'He seems very fond of Maureen, such a sweet child. I look forward to meeting the rest of your family, my dear.'

'I'm sure they're just as eager to meet you, Mevrouw van Doorninck.' Deborah was relieved that they had left the subject of Gerard. 'They're all coming over to spend Christmas.'

'Christmas?' Her companion gave her another sharp look. 'A great deal could happen by then.'

Deborah would have liked to ask her mother-in-law what, in heaven's name, could happen in this well-ordered, well-organised world in which she now lived. A flaming row, she told herself vulgarly, would relieve the monotony, but Gerard was difficult to quarrel with—he became at once blandly courteous, placidly indifferent, a sign, she had decided forlornly, that he didn't consider her of sufficient importance in his life to warrant a loss of temper.

She and Maureen got up to go presently, walking back to the house in the Keizersgracht, to curl up in the comfortable chairs in the sitting room and discuss the delights of Christmas and the not so distant pleasures of the next day when Gerard had promised to take them out.

He telephoned just before dinner, to say that he was detained at the hospital and would dine with a colleague and she wasn't to wait for him. All the same she sat on, long after Maureen had gone to bed and Wim and Marijke had gone to their rooms. But when the clock struck midnight and there was no sign of him, she went to bed too, but not to sleep. She heard his quiet steps going through the quiet house in the early hours of the morning and lay awake until daylight, wondering where he had been and with whom.

He was at breakfast when she got down in the morning, looking, Deborah thought, a little tired but as impeccably dressed as he always was, and although she wanted very much to ask him why he had come home so very late the night before, she held her tongue, remarked on the pleasant morning and read her letters. She was rewarded for this circumspect behaviour by him saying presently:

'I promised to take you both out this afternoon. I'm sorry, but it won't be possible. Could you find something to do, do you suppose?'

She wouldn't let him see her disappointment. 'Of course—there are a hundred and one things on Maureen's list. She'll be disappointed, though.'

'And you.' His glance was thoughtful.

'Oh, I'll be disappointed too; I love sightseeing. As it's her last day, I'll take her to Schevingenen. She'll love it there, and your mother was telling me of a lovely tea-room near the sea.'

She smiled at him, a friendly, casual smile, to let him see that it was of no importance whatever that he had had to cry off, and picked up the rest of her post, only to put it down again as a thought struck her.

'Gerard, would you rather not take Maureen back tomorrow? I can easily take her in the Fiat. Rather a comedown for her after the BMW and the Citroën, I know, but I've been on the road several times now and you said yourself that my driving had improved....'

He frowned at her across the table. 'I don't like the idea of you going that distance, though I must confess that it would be awkward for me to leave.'

'That's settled, then,' she said briskly. 'Only if you don't mind, I think I'll spend a night at home; I don't think I'd be much good at turning round and coming straight back.'

'An excellent idea.' He was still frowning. 'I wonder if there's someone who could drive you— Wim's taking Mother up to Friesland or he could have gone; there may be someone at the hospital.'

'Don't bother,' said Deborah quickly, 'you've enough to do without that. I'll be quite all right, you know, you don't need to give it another thought.'

'Very well, I won't, though if it had been anyone else but you ...'

She was left to decide for herself if he had intended that as a compliment or not.

They were on their way back from Schevingenen that afternoon when she found herself behind her husband's car. He was driving the Citroën, and seated beside him was a small, dark, and very attractive woman, a circumstance which made Deborah thankful that Maureen was so taken up with a large street organ in the opposite direction that she saw nothing.

Presently the traffic allowed her to slip past him. Without looking she was aware of his sudden stare as she raced the little car ahead of the Citroën while Maureen chattered on, still craning her neck to see the last of the organ. Deborah answered her small sister's questions mechanically while her thoughts were busy. So Gerard couldn't spare the time to take them out, though seemingly he had leisure enough to drive around with a pretty woman during an afternoon which was to have been so busy. She had, she told herself savagely, two minds to stay home for a good deal longer than one night. There were, if her memory served her right, several social engagements within the next week or so—let him attend them alone, or better still, with his charming companion. She frowned so fiercely at the very idea that Maureen, turning to speak to her, wanted to know if she had a headache.

Gerard was home for dinner. Deborah greeted him with her usual calm friendliness, hoped that his day hadn't been too busy and plunged into an account of their outing that afternoon, pausing at the end of it to give him time to tell her that he had seen her, and explain his companion. But he said nothing about it at all, only had a short and lively conversation with Maureen and joined her in a game with Smith before shutting himself up in his study.

Deborah exerted herself to be entertaining during dinner, and if her manner was over-bright, her companions didn't seem to notice. After the meal, when Gerard declared himself ready to take Maureen on a boat tour of the lighted canals, even though it was almost dark and getting chilly, she pleaded a headache and stayed at home, working pettishly at a petit-point handbag intended for her mother-in-law's Christmas present.

She and Maureen left after breakfast the next morning to catch the midday ferry from Zeebrugge and Gerard had left the house even earlier; over breakfast he had had very little to say to her, save to advise her to take care and wish her a pleasant journey, but with Maureen he had laughed and joked and given her an enormous box of chocolates as a farewell present and responded suitably to her uninhibited hugs.

They made good time to the ferry, and once on board, repaired to the restaurant where, over her enormous lunch, Maureen talked so much that she didn't notice that Deborah was eating almost nothing.

The drive to Somerset was uneventful. By now the little girl was getting tired; she dozed from time to time, assuring Deborah that she did so only to ensure that she would be wide awake when they reached home. Which left Deborah with her thoughts, running round and round inside her head like mice in a wheel. None of them were happy and all of them were of Gerard.

They reached home at about midnight, to find her parents waiting for them with hot drinks and sandwiches and a host of questions.

Deborah was answering them rather sleepily when the telephone rang and Mr Culpeper, annoyed at the interruption, answered it testily. But his sharp voice shouting, 'Hullo, hullo' in peremptory tones changed to a more friendly accent. 'It's Gerard,' he announced, 'wants to speak to you, Deb.'

She had telephoned the house in Amsterdam on their arrival at Dover, knowing very well that he wouldn't be home and leaving nothing but a brief message with Wim. She picked up the receiver now, schooling her voice to its usual calm and said: 'Hullo, Gerard.'

His voice was quiet and distinct. 'Hullo, Deborah. Wim gave me your message, but I wanted to hear for myself that you had got home safely. I hope I haven't got you out of bed.'

'No. You're up late yourself.'

His 'Yes' was terse. He went on quickly: 'I won't keep you. Have a good night's sleep and drive carefully tomorrow. Good night, Debby.'

She said good night and replaced the receiver. He had never called her Debby before; she wondered about it, but she was really too tired to think. Presently they all went to bed and she slept without waking until she was called in the morning.

She was to take Maureen back to school after breakfast and then continue on her return journey. It seemed lonely after she had left her little sister, still talking and quite revived by a good night's sleep. There hadn't been much time to talk to her mother while she had been home, and perhaps that was a good thing; she might have let slip some small thing ... all the same, it had been a cheerful few hours. Her parents, naturally enough, took it

93

for granted that she was happy and beyond asking after Gerard and agreeing eagerly to the Christmas visit they had said little more; there had been no chance because Maureen had so much to talk about. It would have been nice to have confided in someone, thought Deborah, pushing the little car hard along the road towards the Winchester by-pass, but perhaps not quite loyal to Gerard. The thought of seeing him again made her happy, but the happiness slowly wilted as the day wore on. There had been brilliant sunshine to start with, but now clouds were piling up behind her and long before she reached Dover, it was raining, and out at sea the sky showed a uniform greyness which looked as though it might be there for ever.

She slept for most of the crossing, sitting in a chair in the half-filled ship; she was tired and had been nervous of getting the car on board. Somehow with Maureen she hadn't found it frightening, but going up the steep ramp to the upper car deck she had quaked with fright; it was a relief to sit down for a few hours and recover her cool. She fetched herself a cup of coffee, brought a paperback and settled back. They were within sight of land when she woke and feeling tired still, she tidied herself and after a hasty cup of tea, went to the car deck.

Going down the ramp wasn't too bad, although her engine stalled when she reached the bottom. Deborah found herself trembling as she followed the cars ahead of her towards the Customs booth in the middle of the docks road. Suddenly the drive to Amsterdam didn't seem the easy journey she had made it out to be when she had offered to take Maureen home. It stretched before her in her mind's eye, dark and wet, with the Breskens ferry to negotiate and the long-drawn-out, lonely road across the islands, and Rotterdam ... she had forgotten what a long way it was; somehow she hadn't noticed that when she was with Gerard, or even when she had taken Maureen back, but then it had been broad daylight.

She came to a halt by the Customs, proffered her passport and shivered in the chilly night air as she wound down the window. The man smiled at her. 'You will go to the left, please, Mevrouw.' He waved an arm towards a road leading off from the main docks road.

Deborah was puzzled; all the cars in front of her were keeping straight on. She said slowly so that he would be sure to understand: 'I'm going to Holland—don't I keep straight on to the main road?'

He was still smiling but quite firm. 'To the left, Mevrouw, if you will be so good.'

She went to the left; possibly they were diverting the traffic; she would find out in good time, she supposed. She was going slowly because the arc lights hardly penetrated this smaller side road and she had no idea where it was leading her, nor was there a car in front of her. She was on the point of stopping and going back to make sure that she hadn't misunderstood the Customs man, when her headlights picked out the BMW parked at the side of the road and Gerard leaning against its boot. In the bad light he looked enormous and very reassuring too; she hadn't realized just how much she had wanted to be reassured until she saw him there, standing in the pouring rain, the collar of his Burberry turned up to his ears, a hat pulled down over his eyes. She pulled up then and he walked over to her and when she wound down the window, said: 'Hullo, my dear. I thought it might be a good idea to come and meet you and drive you back—the weather, you know....'

She was still getting over her surprise and joy at seeing him. Her 'hullo' was faint, as was her protesting: 'But I can't leave the Fiat here?'

She became aware that Wim was there too, standing discreetly in the background by his master's car. Gerard nodded towards him. 'I brought Wim with me, he'll take the Fiat back.' He opened the car door. 'Come along, Deborah, we shall be home in no time at all.'

She got out silently and allowed herself to be tucked up snugly beside him in the BMW, pausing only to greet Wim and hope that he didn't mind driving the Fiat home.

'A pleasure, Mevrouw,' grinned Wim cheerfully, 'but I think that you will be there first.' He put out a hand to take the car keys from her and raised it in salute as he walked back to her car.

As Gerard reversed his own car and swept back the way she had come Deborah asked: 'Oh, is that why he told me to come this way and not out of the main gate?'

'Yes—I was afraid that we might miss you once you got past the Customs. Did you have a good trip back?'

For a variety of reasons and to her great shame her voice was drowned in a sudden flood of tears. She swallowed them back frantically and they poured down her cheeks instead. She stared out of the window at the outskirts of the town—flat land, dotted here and there with houses, it looked untidy even in the dim light of the overhead street lamps—and willed herself to be calm. After a minute Gerard said 'Deborah?' and because she would have to say something sooner or later she managed a 'Yes, thank you,' and spoilt it with a dreary snivel.

He slid the car to the side of the road on to a patch of waste land and switched off the engine. He had tossed off his hat when he got into the car; now he turned his handsome head and looked down at her in the semi-dark. 'What happened?' he asked gently, and then: 'Debby, I've never seen you cry before.'

She sniffed, struggled to get herself under control and managed:

'I hardly ever do—n-nothing's the m-matter, it's just that I'm tired, I expect.' She added on a small wail: 'I was t-terrified—those ramps on the ferry, they were ghastly—I thought I'd never reach the top and I didn't notice with Maureen, but when I was by m-myself it was awful, and the engine stalled and it was raining and when I got off the ferry it s-seemed s-such a long way to get home.' She hiccoughed, blew her nose and mopped her wet cheeks.

'I should never have let you go alone, I must have been mad. My poor girl, what a thoughtless man I am! You see, you are—always have been—so calm and efficient and able to cope, and then last night when I telephoned you, you sounded so tired —I rearranged my work to come and meet you. I remembered this long dark road too, Deborah, and in the Fiat it would be even longer. Forgive me, Deborah.'

She sniffed. His arm, flung along the back of the seat and holding her shoulders lightly, was comforting, and she was rapidly regaining her self-control. Later, she knew, she would be furious with herself for breaking down in this stupid fashion. She said in a voice which was nearly normal: 'Thank you very much, Gerard. It was only because it was raining and so very dark.'

She felt his arm slide away. 'I've some coffee here —Marijke always regards any journey more than ten miles distant from Amsterdam as being fraught with danger and probable starvation and provides accordingly. Sandwiches, too.'

They ate and drank in a companionable silence and presently Gerard began to talk, soothing nothings about her parents and her home and Smith— perhaps he talked to his more nervous patients like that, she thought sleepily, before he told them that he would have to operate. He took her cup from her presently and said: 'Go to sleep, Deborah, there's nothing to look at at this time of night—I'll wake you when we reach Amsterdam.'

She started to tell him that she wasn't tired any more, and fell asleep saying it.

She wakened to the touch of his hand on her arm. 'A few minutes,' he told her, and she was astonished to see the still lighted, now familiar streets of the city all around them. But the Keizersgracht was only dimly lit, its water gleaming dimly through the bare trees lining the road. It was still raining, but softly now, and there were a few lights from the houses they passed. As they drew up before their own front door, she saw that the great chandelier in the hall was beaming its light through the glass transom over the door and the sitting room was lighted too so that the wet pavement glistened in its glow. Gerard helped her out of the car and took her arm and they crossed the cobbles together as the front door was flung open and Marijke, with a wildly barking Smith, stood framed within it.

Going through the door Deborah knew at that moment just how much she loved the old house; it welcomed her, just as Marijke and Smith were welcoming her, as though she had returned from a long and arduous journey. She smiled a little mistily at Marijke and bent to catch Smith up into her arms. They went into the sitting room and Gerard took her coat, then Marijke was there almost at once with more hot coffee and a plate of paper-thin sandwiches. She talked volubly to Gerard while she set them out on the silver tray and carried it over to put on the table by Deborah's chair. When she had gone, Deborah asked: 'What was all that about?'

He came to sit opposite her and now she could see the lines of fatigue on his face, so that before he could answer she asked: 'Have you had a hard day?'

He smiled faintly. 'Yes.'

'You've been busy—too busy, lately.'

'That is no excuse for letting you go all that way alone.'

She said firmly: 'It was splendid for my driving. I'll not mind again.'

'There won't be an again,' he told her briefly, 'and Marijke was talking about you.'

'Oh—I recognised one word—stomach.'

It was nice to see him laugh like that. 'She said that you look tired and that beautiful women should never look other than beautiful. She strongly advised nourishment for your—er—stomach so that you would sleep like a rose.'

Deborah said softly: 'What a charming thing to

say, about the rose, I mean. Dear Marijke—she and Wim, they're like the house, aren't they?' And was sorry that she had said it, because he might not understand. But he did; the look he gave her was one of complete understanding. She smiled at him and then couldn't look away from his intent gaze. 'You saw me the other afternoon,' he stated the fact simply. 'You have been wondering why I couldn't find the time to take you and Maureen on a promised trip and yet have the leisure to drive around with a very attractive woman—she was attractive, did you not think so?'

'Yes.'

'I don't discuss my patients with you, you know that, I think—although I must confess I have frequently wished to do so—but I do not wish you to misunderstand. The patient upon whom I operated the other evening was. . . .' he named someone and Deborah sat up with a jerk, although she said nothing. 'Yes, you see why I have been so worried and—secretive. The lady with me was his wife. She had been to Schiphol to meet her daughter, who was breaking her journey on her way home to get news of her father. At the last moment his wife declared that she was unable to tell her and asked me to do it. We were on our way back to the hospital when you saw us. I should have told you sooner. I'm not sure why I didn't, perhaps I was piqued at the way you ignored the situation. Any other woman—wife—would have asked.'

'It was none of my business,' she said stiffly. 'I didn't know. . . .'

'You mean that you suspected me of having a girl-friend?' He was smiling, but she sensed his controlled anger.

There was no point in being anything but honest with him. 'Yes, I think I did, but it still wouldn't be my business, and it shouldn't matter, should it?'

He hadn't taken his eyes off her. 'I believe you said that once before. You think that? But do you not know me well enough to know that I would have been quite honest with you before I married you?'

Her head had begun to ache. 'Oh, yes, indeed, but that wasn't what I meant. What I'm trying to say is that I've no right to mind, have I?'

Gerard got to his feet and pulled her gently to hers. 'You have every right in the world,' he assured her. 'I don't think our bargain included that kind of treatment of each other, Deborah. I don't cheat the people I like.'

She didn't look at him. 'No, I know that, truly I do. I'm sorry I was beastly. I think I'm tired.'

They walked together out of the room and in the hall he kissed her cheek. 'I'll wait for Wim, he shouldn't be much longer now. And by the way, I've taken some time off. In a couple of days I'll take you to the house in Friesland, and we might go and see some friends of mine who live close by—she's English, too.'

Deborah was half way up the stairs. 'That sounds lovely,' she told him and then turned round to say: 'Thank you for coming all that way, it must have been a bind after a hard day's work.'

He didn't answer her, but she was conscious of his eyes on her as she climbed the stairs.

CHAPTER SIX

But before they went to Friesland Deborah met some other friends of Gerard's. She had spent a quiet day after her return, arranging the menu for a dinner party they were to give during the following week, paying a morning visit to her mother-in-law, telephoning her own mother and writing a few letters before taking Smith for a walk. She was back home, waiting for Gerard's return from the Grotehof after tea, when the telephone rang.

It was a woman's voice, light and sweet, enquiring if Mijnheer van Doorninck was home. 'No,' said Deborah, and wondered who it was, 'I'm sorry —perhaps I could take a message?' She spoke in the careful Dutch the professor had taught her, and hoped that the conversation wasn't going to get too involved.

'Is that Gerard's wife?' asked the voice, in English now, and when Deborah said a little uncertainly: 'Why, yes——' went on: 'Oh, good. I'm Adelaide van Essen. My husband's paediatrician at the Grotehof and a friend of Gerard. We got back from England last night and Coenraad telephoned me just now and told me about you. You don't mind me ringing you up?'

'I'm delighted—I don't know any English people here yet.'

'Well, come and meet me—us, for a start. Come this evening. I know it's short notice, but I told Coenraad to ask Gerard to bring you to dinner—you will come?'

'I'd love to.' Deborah paused. 'I'm not sure about Gerard, he works late quite a lot and often works at home.'

She had the impression that the girl at the other end of the line was concealing surprise. Then: 'I'm sure he'll make time. We haven't seen each other for ages and the men are old friends. We live quite near you, in the Herengracht—is seven o'clock too early? Oh, and here's our number in case you want to ring back. Till seven, then. I'm so looking forward to meeting you.'

Deborah went back to her chair. The voice had sounded nice, soft and gentle and friendly. She spent the next ten minutes or so in deciding what she should wear and still hadn't made up her mind when Gerard came in.

His hullo was friendly and after he had enquired about her day, he took a chair near her. 'I met a friend of mine at the Grotehof this afternoon,' he told her, 'Coenraad van Essen—he's married to an English girl. They're just back from England and they want us to go round for dinner this evening. Would you like to go? It's short notice and I don't know if it will upset any arrangements you may have made?'

She chose a strand of silk and threaded her needle. 'His wife telephoned a few minutes ago. I'd like to go very much. She suggested seven o'clock, so I had better go and talk to Marijke.'

Marijke hadn't started the cutlets and the cheese soufflé; Deborah, in her laborious Dutch and helped by a few words here and there from Wim, suggested that they should have them the following day instead and apologised for the short notice. To which Marijke had a whole lot to say in reply, her face all smiles. Deborah turned to Wim. 'I don't quite understand. . . .'

'Marijke is saying that it is good for you to see a lady of your own age and also English. She wishes you a merry evening.' He beamed at her. 'Me, I wish the same also, Mevrouw.'

She wore the pink silk jersey dress she had been unable to resist the last time she had visited Metz, the fashionable dress shop within walking distance of the house, and went downstairs to find Gerard waiting for her, 'I'm not late?' she asked anxiously as she crossed the hall.

'No—I wanted a few minutes with you. Shall we go into the sitting room?'

Deborah's heart dropped to her elegant shoes. What was he going to tell her? That he was going away on one of his teaching trips—that he wouldn't be able to take her to Friesland after all? She arranged her face into a suitable composure and turned to face him.

'Did you never wonder why I had not given you a wedding gift?' he asked her. 'Not because I had given no thought to it; there were certain alterations I wanted done, and only today are they finished.'

He took a small velvet case from his pocket and opened it. There were earrings inside on its thick satin lining; elaborate pearl drops in a diamond setting. She looked at them with something like awe. 'My goodness,' she uttered, 'they're—they're beautiful! I've never seen anything like them.'

He had taken them from their box. 'Try them on,' he invited her. 'They're very old, but the setting was clumsy; I've had them re-set to my own design. You are tall enough to take such a style, I think.'

She had gone to the mirror over the sofa table and

hooked them in and stood looking at them. They were exquisite, and he was right, they suited her admirably. She turned her lovely head and watched the diamonds take fire. 'I don't know how to thank you,' she began. 'They're magnificent!'

Thanking him didn't seem quite enough, so she went to him and rather hesitantly kissed his cheek. 'Do you suppose I might wear them this evening?' she asked.

'Why not?' He had gone over to the small secretaire by one of the windows and was opening one of its drawers. He returned with another, larger case in his hand. 'This has been in the family for quite some time too,' he observed as he gave it to her. 'I've had it re-strung and the clasp re-set to match the earrings.'

Deborah opened the case slowly. There were pearls in it, a double row with a diamond and pearl clasp which followed the exact pattern of the earrings. She stared at it and all she could manage was an ecstatic 'Oh!' Gerard took them from her and fastened them round her neck and she went back to the mirror and had another look; they were quite superb. 'I don't know how to thank you,' she repeated, quite at a loss for words. 'It's the most wonderful wedding present anyone could dream of having.'

He was standing behind her, staring at her reflection. After a moment he smiled faintly. 'You are my wife,' he pointed out. 'You are entitled to them.' He spoke lightly as he turned away.

He need not have said that, she thought unhappily, looking at her suddenly downcast face in the mirror. It took her a few moments to fix a smile on to it before she turned away and picked up her coat.

'Do we walk or go in the car?' she asked brightly.

He helped her into her coat and she could have been his sister, she thought bitterly, for all the impression she made upon him. 'The car,' he told her cheerfully. 'It's almost seven, perhaps we had better go at once.'

The house in the Herengracht was bigger than Gerard's but very similar in style. Its vast front door was opened as they reached it and an elderly man greeted them with a 'Good evening, Mevrouw —Mijnheer.'

Gerard slapped him on the shoulder. 'Tweedle, how are you? You haven't called me Mijnheer for many a long day.' He looked at Deborah, smiling. 'This is Tweedle, my dear, who has been with Coenraad since he was a toddler. I daresay you will meet Mrs Tweedle presently.'

'Indeed, she will be delighted,' Tweedle informed them gravely, adding: 'The Baron and Baroness are in the small sitting room, Mr Gerard.'

He led the way across the panelled hall and opened a door, announcing them as he did so, and Deborah, with Gerard's hand under her elbow urging her gently on, went in.

The room was hardly small and she saw at a glance that it was furnished with some magnificent pieces worthy of a museum, yet it was decidedly lived in; there was a mass of knitting cast down carelessly on a small drum table, a pile of magazines were tumbled on to the sofa table behind the big settee before the chimneypiece, and there was a pleasant scent of flowers, tobacco and—very faint— beeswax polish. There were two people in the room, a man as tall as Gerard but somewhat older, his dark hair greying at the temples, horn-rimmed glasses astride his handsome beaky nose. It was a kind face as well as a good-looking one, and Deborah decided then and there that she was going to like Gerard's friend. The girl who got up with him was small, slim and very pretty, with huge dark eyes and a mass of bright red hair piled high. She was wearing a very simple dress of cream silk and some of the loveliest sapphires Deborah had ever set eyes on. She felt Gerard's hand on her arm again and went forward to receive the baron's quiet welcome and the charming enthusiasm of his small wife, who, after kissing Gerard in a sisterly fashion, led her to a small sofa and sat down beside her.

'You really are a dear to come at a moment's notice,' she declared. 'You didn't mind?'

Deborah shook her head, smiling. She was going to like this small vivid creature. 'It was kind of you to ask us. I'm so glad to meet another English girl. Gerard has been so busy and—and we haven't been married very long. I've met a great many of his colleagues, though.'

Her companion glanced at her quickly. 'Duty dinners,' she murmured, 'and the rest of the time they're immersed in their work. Coenraad says you were Gerard's Theatre Sister.'

'Yes. I worked for him for two years while he was at Clare's.' She felt she should have been able to say more about it than that, but she could think of nothing. There was a pause before her hostess asked: 'Do you like Amsterdam? I love it. We've a house in Dorset and we go there whenever we can, and to my parents, of course. The children love it.'

She didn't look old enough to have children.

'How many have you?' Deborah asked.

'Two.' Adelaide turned to take the drink her husband was offering her and he corrected her smilingly: 'Two and a half, my love.'

Deborah watched him exchange a loving glance, full of content and happiness, and swallowed envy as she heard her host say: 'Do you hear that, Gerard? You're going to be a godfather again—some time in the New Year.' And when Gerard joined them, he added: 'We'll do the same for you, of course.'

Everyone laughed; this was the sort of occasion, Deborah told herself bitterly, that she hadn't reckoned with. She made haste to ask the children's names and was at once invited to visit them in their beds.

'They won't be asleep,' their doting mother assured her, 'at least Champers won't. Lisa's only eighteen months old and drops off in seconds. Champers likes to lie and think.'

She led the way up the curving staircase and into the night nursery where an elderly woman was tidying away a pile of clothes. She was introduced as Nanny Best, the family treasure, before she trotted softly away with a bright nod. The two girls went to the cot first; the small girl in it was a miniature of her mother, the same fiery hair and preposterous lashes, the same small nose. She was asleep, her mother dropped a kiss on one fat pink cheek and crossed the room to the small bed against the opposite wall. There was no doubt at all that the small boy in it was the baron's son. Here was the dark hair, the beaky nose and the calm expression. He grinned widely at his mother, offered a hand to Deborah and after kissing them both good night, declared his intention of going to sleep.

They went back downstairs and were met in the hall by the Labrador dogs. 'Castor and Pollux,' Adelaide introduced them, and tucked an arm into Deborah's. 'Call me Adelaide,' she begged in her sweet voice. 'I'm going to call you Deborah.' She paused to look at her companion. 'You're quite beautiful, you know, no wonder Gerard married you.' Her eyes lingered on the earrings. 'I like these,' she said, touching them with a gentle finger, 'and the pearls, they suit you. How lucky you are to be tall and curvy, you can wear all the jewels Gerard will doubtless give you, but look at me— one pearl necklace and I'm smothered!'

They laughed together as they entered the room and the two men looked up. Coenraad said: 'There you are, darling—do you girls want another drink before dinner?'

The meal was a splendid one. Deborah, looking round the large, well appointed dining room, reflected how well the patrician families lived with their large old houses, their priceless antique furniture, their china and glass and silver and most important of all, their trusted servants who were devoted to them and looked after their possessions with as much pride as that of their owners.

She was recalled to her surroundings by Adelaide. 'So you're going to Friesland,' she commented. 'I expect Gerard will take you to see Dominic and Abigail—she's English, too—they live close by. They're both dears. They've a house in Amsterdam, of course, but they go to Friesland when they can. Abigail is expecting a baby in about six months.' She grinned happily. 'Won't it be fun, all of us living near enough to pop in and visit, and so nice for the children—they can all play together.'

Deborah agreed, aware that Gerard had stopped talking and was listening too. 'What are the schools like?' she heard herself ask in a voice which sounded as though she really wanted to know.

They stayed late; when they got back home the house was quiet, for Wim and Marijke had long since gone to bed, but the great chandelier in the hall still blazed and there were a couple of lamps invitingly lighting the sitting room. Deborah wandered in and perched on the side of a chair.

'You enjoyed the evening?' Gerard wanted to know, following her.

'Very much—what a nice person Adelaide is, and so is Coenraad. I hope I did the right thing, I asked them to join our dinner party next week.'

'Splendid. Coenraad and I have known each other for a very long time.' He went on: 'He and Addy are very devoted.'

'Yes.' Deborah didn't want to talk about that, it hurt too much. 'I'm looking forward to meeting Abigail too.'

'Ah, yes, on Saturday. We'll leave fairly early in the morning, shall we, go to the house first and then go on to Dominic's place in the afternoon. Probably they'll want us to stay for dinner, but as I'm not going in to the Grotehof in the morning, it won't matter if we're late back.'

She got up. 'It sounds delightful. I think I'll go to bed.' She put a hand up to the pearl necklace. 'Thank you again for my present, Gerard. I'll treasure it, and the earrings.'

He was switching off the lamps. 'But of course,' he told her blandly. 'They have been treasured for generations of van Doorninck brides, and I hope will continue to be treasured for a long time to come.'

She went upstairs wondering why he had to remind her so constantly that married though they were, she was an—she hesitated for a word—outsider.

Deborah half expected that something would turn up to prevent them going to Friesland, but it didn't. They left soon after eight o'clock, travelling at a great pace through Hoorn and Den Oever and over the Afsluitdijk and so into Friesland. Once on the land again, Gerard turned the car away from the Leeuwarden road, to go through Bolsward and presently Sneek and into the open country beyond. Deborah was enchanted with what she saw; there seemed to be water everywhere.

'Do you sail at all?' she wanted to know of Gerard.

He slowed the car and turned into a narrow road running along the top of a dyke. He looked years younger that morning, perhaps because he was wearing slacks and a sweater with a gay scarf tucked in its neck, perhaps because he had a whole day in which to do as he liked.

'I've a small yacht, a van der Stadt design, around ten tons displacement—she sails like a dream.'

She wasn't sure what ten tons displacement meant. 'Where do you keep her?'

'Why, at Domwier—I can sail her down the canal to the lake. I've had no time this summer to do much sailing, though, and it's getting late in the year now, though with this lovely autumn we might have a chance—would you like to come with me?'

'Oh, please, if I wouldn't be a nuisance; I don't know a thing about boats, but I'm willing to learn.'

'Good—that's a dare, if the weather holds. We're almost at Domwier—it's a very small village; a church, a shop and a handful of houses. The house is a mile further on.'

The sun sparkled on the lake as they approached it, the opposite shore looked green and pleasant with its trees and thickets, even though there weren't many leaves left. They drove through a thick curtain of birch and pine and saw the lake, much nearer now, beyond rough grass. She barely had time to look at it before Gerard turned into a short sandy lane and there was the house before them. It looked like a farmhouse without the barn behind it, built square and solid with no-nonsense windows and an outsize door surmounted by a carving of two white swans. The sweep before the house was bordered by flower beds, still colourful with dahlias and chrysanthemums, and beyond them, grass and a thick screen of trees and bushes through which she glimpsed the water again. Smith tumbled out of the car to tear round the garden, barking ecstatically, while they made their way rather more soberly to the front door. It stood open on to a tiled hall with a door on either side and another at its end through which came a stout woman, almost as tall as Gerard. That she was delighted to see them was obvious, although Deborah could discover nothing of what she was saying. It was only when Gerard said: 'Forgive us, we're speaking Fries, because Sien dislikes speaking anything else,' that she realised that they were speaking another language altogether. Her heart sank a little; now she would have to learn this language too! As though he had read her thoughts, Gerard added: 'Don't worry, you won't be expected to speak it, though Sien would love you for ever if you could learn to understand just a little of what she says.'

'Then I'll do that, I promise. Do you come up here often?'

He corrected her gently: 'We shall, I hope, come up here often. Once things are exactly as I want them at the hospital, I shall have a good deal more time. I have been away for two years, remember, with only brief visits.'

'Yes, I know, but must you work so hard every day? I mean, you're not often home...' She wished she hadn't said it, for she sensed his withdrawal.

'I'm afraid you must accept that, Deborah.' He was smiling nicely, but his eyes were cool. He turned back to Sien and said something to her and she shook Deborah's hand and, still talking, went back to the kitchen.

Gerard flung an arm round Deborah's shoulders and led her to the sitting room. 'Coffee,' he invited her, 'and then we'll go round the place.' His manner was friendly, just as though he had forgotten their slight discord.

The room was simply furnished in the traditional Friesian style, with painted cupboards against the walls, rush-seated chairs, a stove with a tiled surround and a nicely balanced selection of large, comfortable chairs. There was a telephone too and a portable television tucked discreetly in a corner. 'It's simple,' Gerard had seen her glance, 'but we have comfort and convenience.'

113

Most decidedly, she agreed silently, as Sien came in with a heavy silver tray with its accompanying silver pot and milk jug and delicate cups. The coffee was delicious and so was the spiced cake which accompanied it. They sat over it and Deborah, determined to keep the conversation on safe ground, asked questions about the house and the furniture and the small paintings hung each side of the stove. She found them enchanting, just as beautiful in their way as the priceless portraits in the Amsterdam house; the ancestors who had sat for Paulus Potter, the street scene by Hendrik Sorgh and the two by Gerrit Berckheyde; she had admired them greatly, almost nervous of the fact that she was now in part responsible for them. But these delicate sketches and paintings were much smaller and perfect to the last hair and whisker—fieldmice mostly, small animals of all kinds, depicted with a precise detail which she found amazing.

'They're by Jacob de Gheyn,' Gerard told her. 'An ancestress of mine loved small animals, so her husband commissioned these for her, and they have been there ever since. I agree with you, they're quite delightful. Come and see the rest of the house.'

The dining room was on the other side of the hall, with a great square bay window built out to take in the view of the lake beyond, comfortably furnished with enormous chairs covered in bright patterned damask. There was a Dutch dresser against one wall, decked with enormous covered tureens and rows of old Delftware. There was a similar dresser in the kitchen too which Deborah could see was as up-to-date as the latest model at the Ideal Home Exhibition, and upstairs the two bathrooms, tiled and cosily carpeted, each with its pile of brightly coloured towels and a galaxy of matching soaps and powders, rivalled the luxury of the town house. By contrast the bedrooms were simply furnished while still offering every comfort, even the two small attic rooms, reached by an almost perpendicular flight of miniature stairs, were as thickly carpeted and as delightfully furnished as the large rooms on the floor below.

As they went downstairs again she said a little shyly: 'This is a lovely house, Gerard—how wonderful to come here when you want peace and quiet. I love the house in Amsterdam, but I could love this one as much.'

He gave her an approving glance. 'You feel that? I'm glad, I have a great fondness for it. Mother too, she comes here frequently. It's quiet in the winter, of course.'

'I think I should like it then—does the lake freeze over?'

They had strolled into the dining room and found Sien busy putting the finishing touches to the lunch table. 'Yes, though not always hard enough for skating. I can remember skating across to Dominic's house during some of the really cold winters, though.'

'But it's miles....'

He poured her a glass of sherry. 'Not quite. Round about a mile, I should suppose. We shall have to drive back to the road presently, of course, and go round the head of the lake. It's no distance.'

They set off after a lunch which Deborah had thoroughly enjoyed because Gerard had been amusing and gay and relaxed; and she had never felt so close, and she wondered if he felt it too. It was on the tip of her tongue to try and explain a little to him of how she felt—oh, not to tell him that she loved him; she had the good sense to see that such a statement would cook her goose for ever, but to let him see, if she could, that she was happy and contented and anxious to please him. But there was no chance to say any of these things; they left immediately after lunch and the journey was too short to start a serious talk.

Dominic's house, when they reached it, was a good deal larger than their own but furnished in a similar style. Dominic had come to meet them as they got out of the car, his arm around his wife's shoulders. He was another large man. Deborah found him attractive and almost as good-looking as Gerard, and as for his wife, she was a small girl who would have been plain if happiness hadn't turned her into a beauty. She shook hands now and said in a pretty voice:

'This is a lovely surprise—we heard that Gerard had married and we had planned to come and see you when we got back to Amsterdam. We were returning this week, but the weather's so marvellous, and once the winter starts it goes on and on.'

Inside they talked until tea came, and presently when Gerard suggested that they should go, there was no question of it. 'You'll stay to dinner,' said Abigail. 'Besides,' and now she was smiling, 'I mustn't be thwarted, because of my condition.' There was a general laugh and she turned to Deborah. 'Well, I'm not the only one, I hear Adelaide van Essen is having another baby—isn't she a dear?'

Deborah agreed. 'It's wonderful to find some

other English girls living so close by.' She added hastily, 'Not that I'm lonely, but I find Dutch rather difficult, though I am having lessons.'

'Professor de Wit?' asked Abigail. 'Adelaide went to him. I nursed his brother before I married Dominic.' The two girls plunged into an interesting chat which was only broken by Dominic suggesting mildly that perhaps Abigail should let Bollinger know that there would be two more for dinner.

Abigail got up. 'Oh, darling, I forgot. Deborah, come and meet Bolly—he came over from England with me, and he's part of the household now.'

She smiled at her husband as they left the room, and Deborah, seeing it, felt a pang of sadness. It seemed that everyone else but herself and Gerard was happily married. Walking to the kitchen, half listening to Abigail's happy voice, she wondered if she had tried hard enough, or perhaps she had tried too much. Perhaps she annoyed him in some way, or worse, bored him. She would have to know. She resolved to ask him.

She did so, buoyed up by a false courage induced by Dominic's excellent wine. They were half way home, tearing along the Afsluitdijk with no traffic problems to occupy him.

'Do I bore you, Gerard?' she asked, and heard the small sound he made. Annoyance? Impatience? Surprise, perhaps.

But when he answered her his voice was as cool and casually friendly as usual. 'Not in the least. What put such an idea into your head?'

'N-nothing. I just wondered if you were quite satisfied—I mean with our marriage; if I'm being the kind of wife you wanted. You see, we're not much together and I don't know a great deal about you—perhaps when you get home in the evening and you're tired you'd rather be left in peace with the paper and a drink. I wouldn't mind a bit....'

They were almost at the end of the dyke, approaching the great sluices at its end. Gerard slowed down and gave her a quick look in the dark of the car.

He said on a laugh: 'I do believe you're trying to turn me into a Dutchman with my gin and my paper after a hard day's work!' His voice changed. 'I'm quite satisfied, Deborah. You are the wife I wanted, you certainly don't bore me, I'm always glad to see you when I get home, however tired I am.' His voice became kind. 'Surely that is enough to settle your doubts?'

Quite enough, she told him silently, and quite hopeless too. An irrational desire to drum her heels on the floorboards and scream loudly took possession of her. She overcame it firmly. 'Yes, thank you, Gerard,' and began at once to talk about the house in Friesland. The subject was threadbare by the time they reached Amsterdam, but at least she had managed not to mention themselves again.

It was late and she went straight to bed, leaving Gerard to take Smith for his last perambulation and lock up, and in the morning when she came down it was to hear from Wim that he had been called to the hospital in the very early morning and hadn't returned. It was almost lunchtime when he did, and as his mother had been invited for that meal, it was impossible to ask him about it; in any case, even if they had been alone, he would probably not have told her anything. She applied herself to her mother-in-law's comfort and after lunch sat in the drawing room with her, listening to tales of the family and making suitable comments from time to time, all the while wondering where Gerard had got to. He had gone to his study—she knew that, because he had said that he had a telephone call to make, but that was more than two hours ago. The two ladies had tea together and Deborah had just persuaded the older lady to stay to dinner when Gerard joined them with the hope that they had spent a pleasant afternoon and never a word about his own doings.

He told her the reason for his absence that evening after he had driven his mother back to her flat.

'Before you ask me any of the questions I feel sure are seething inside your head, I'll apologise most humbly.'

'Apologise? Whatever for?' She put down the book she had been reading and stared at him in astonishment.

'Leaving you with Mother for the entire afternoon.'

'But you had some calls to make—some work to do, didn't you?'

He grinned suddenly and her heart thumped against her ribs because he looked as she knew he might look if he were happy and carefree and not chained to the hospital by chains of his own forging. 'I went to sleep.' And when she goggled at him: 'I know, I'm sorry, but the fact is, I had some work to do after we got home last night and I stayed up until two o'clock or thereabouts, and I had to go to the Grotehof for an emergency op at five.'

'Gerard, you must have been worn out! Why on earth didn't you tell me, why won't you let me help you. . . .' That wouldn't do at all, so she went on briskly: 'And there was I telling your mother that you never had a minute to call your own, working at your desk even on a Sunday afternoon.'

He was staring hard at her. 'You're a loyal wife,' he said quietly, and she flushed faintly under his eyes.

'I expect all wives are,' she began, and saw the expression on his face. It had become remote again; he was remembering Sasja, she supposed, who hadn't been loyal at all. 'Shall we have dinner early tomorrow evening so that you can get your work done in good time? Have you a heavy list in the morning?'

'That was something I was going to tell you. I've changed the list to the afternoon—two o'clock, because I thought we might go for a run in the morning.'

A little colour crept into her cheeks again, but she kept her voice as ordinary as possible. 'That sounds nice. Where shall we go?'

'Not too far. The river Vecht, perhaps—we could keep off the motorway and there won't be much traffic about this time of the year.'

Deborah agreed happily, and later, in bed, thinking about it, she dared to hope that perhaps Gerard's first rigid ideas about their marriage weren't as rigid as they had been. She slept peacefully on that happy thought.

They were out of Amsterdam by nine o'clock the next morning, driving through the crisp autumn air. Gerard took the road to Naarden and then turned off on to the narrow road following the Vecht, going slowly so that Deborah could inspect the houses on its banks, built by the merchant princes in the eighteenth century, and because she found them so fascinating he obligingly turned the car at the end of the road and drove back again the same way, patiently answering her questions about them. They had coffee in Loenen and because there was still plenty of time before they had to return to Amsterdam he didn't follow the road to Naarden again, but turned off into the byroads which would lead them eventually back to the city.

The road they were on stretched apparently unending between the flat fields, and save for a group of farm cottages half a mile away, and ahead of them the vague outline of a farmhouse, there was nothing moving except a farm tractor being driven across a ploughed field. Deborah watched the driver idly as they came level with him. 'He must be lonely,' she said idly, and then urgently: 'Gerard, that tractor's going to turn over!'

She was glad that he wasn't one of those men who asked needless questions; they weren't travelling fast, so he slid to a halt and had the door open as the tractor, some way off, reared itself up like an angry monster and crashed down on to its hapless driver.

Even in his hurry, it warmed Deborah's heart when Gerard leaned across her to undo her door and snap back her safety belt so that she could get out quickly. There was a narrow ditch between the road and the field; he bridged it easily with his long legs and then turned to give her a hand before they started to run as best they might across the newly turned earth.

The man had made no sound. When they reached him he was unconscious, trapped by the bonnet of the tractor, its edge biting across the lower half of his body.

It was like being back in theatre, thought Deborah wildly, working in a silent agreed pattern which needed no speech. She found a pulse and counted it with care while Gerard's hands began a careful search over the man's body.

'Nasty crack on his head on this side,' she offered, and peered at the eyes under their closed lids. 'Pupil reaction is equal.'

Gerard grunted, his fingers probing and feeling and probing again.

'I'm pretty sure his pelvis is fractured, God knows what's happened to his legs—how's his pulse?' She told him and he nodded. 'Not too bad,' and examined more closely the wound on the man's head. 'Can't feel a fracture, though I think there may be a crack. We've got to get this thing eased off him, even if it's only a centimetre.'

He slid a powerful arm as far as it would go and heaved with great caution and slowness. 'Half an inch would do it.' He was talking to himself. 'Your belt, Debby—if we could budge this thing just a shade and stuff your belt in. . . .'

She had her belt off while he was still speaking. 'How about trying to scoop the earth from under him and slip the belt in?'

He had understood her at once. He crouched beside the man, the belt in his hand, his arm ready to thrust it between the bonnet's rim and the man's body. Deborah dug with speedy calm; there was nothing to use but her hands. She felt the nails crack and tear and saw, in a detached way, the front of her expensive tweed two-piece gradually disappear under an encrustation of damp earth,

122

but presently she was able to say: 'Try now, Gerard.'

It worked, albeit the pressure was eased fractionally and wouldn't last long. Gerard withdrew his arm with great care and said: 'We have to get help.' His voice was as calm as though he was commenting upon the weather. 'Take the keys and drive the car to that farm we saw ahead of us and ask ... no, that'll take too long, I'll go. Stay here—there's nothing much you can do. Push the belt in further if you get the chance.' He got to his feet. 'Thank heaven you're a strapping girl with plenty of strength and common sense!'

He started to run back towards the car, leaving her smouldering; did he really regard her as strapping? He had made her sound like some muscly creature with no feminine attributes at all! Deborah chuckled and the chuckle changed to a sob which she sternly swallowed; now was no time to be feminine. She took the man's pulse once more and wondered how long she would have to wait before Gerard got back.

Not long—she saw the car racing down the road and prayed silently that there would be nothing in the way. The next minutes seemed like eternity. Deborah turned her head at length to see Gerard with four or five men, coming towards her. They were carrying ropes and when he was near enough she said in the matter-of-fact voice he would expect of her: 'His pulse is going up, but it's steady. What are you going to do?'

'Get ropes round this infernal thing and try and drag it off.'

'You'll get double hernias,' she warned him seriously.

Gerard gave a crack of laughter. 'A risk we must all take. I fear, there's no other tractor for miles around.'

He turned away from her and became immersed in the task before him. They had the ropes in place and were heaving on them steadily when the first police car arrived, disgorging two men to join the team of sweating, swearing men. The tractor shuddered and rolled over with a thud, leaving the man free just as the second police car and an ambulance arrived.

Gerard scarcely heeded them; he was on his knees, examining the man's legs. 'By some miracle,' he said quietly to Deborah, 'they're not pulped. I may be able to do something about them provided we can get at him quickly enough. Get me some splints.'

She went to meet the ambulance men making all the speed they could over the soft earth. She had no idea what the word splint was in Dutch, but luckily they were carrying an armful, so she took several from one rather astonished man, smiled at him and raced back to Gerard. He took them without a word and then said: 'Good lord, girl, what am I supposed to tie them with?'

She raced back again and this time the ambulance man ran to meet her and kept beside her as she ran back with the calico slings. There was help enough now, she stood back and waited patiently. It took a long time to get the man on to the stretcher and carry him, with infinite caution across the field to the waiting ambulance. She waited until the little procession had reached it before following it and when she reached the car there was no sign of Gerard, so she got in and sat waiting with the patience she had learned during her years of nursing. The ambulance drove off presently and one of the policemen leaned through the car window and proffered her a note—from Gerard, scribbled in his almost undecipherable scrawl. 'I must go with the ambulance to the Grotehof,' he had written on a sheet torn out of his pocket book. 'Drive the car back and wait in the hospital courtyard.' He had signed it 'G' and added a postscript: 'The BMW is just like the Fiat, only larger.'

All the same, reading these heartening words, Deborah felt a pang of nervousness; she had never driven the BMW; if she thought about it for too long she would be terrified of doing so. She thanked the policeman who saluted politely, and happily ignorant of the fact that she was almost sick with fright, drove away. It was quite five minutes before she could summon up the courage to press the self-starter.

She was still shaking when she stopped the car cautiously before the entrance to the hospital, wondering what she was supposed to do next. But Gerard had thought of that; Deborah was sitting back in her seat, taking a few calming breaths when the Medical Ward Sister, whom she had already met, popped her head through the window. 'Mevrouw van Doorninck, you will come with me, please.'

'Hullo,' said Deborah, and then: 'Why, Zuster?'

'It is the wish of Mijnheer van Doorninck.' Her tone implied that there was sufficient reason there without the need for any more questions.

'Where is he?' asked Deborah, sitting stubbornly where she was.

'In theatre, already scrubbed. But he wishes most

earnestly that you will come with me.' She added plaintively: 'I am so busy, Mevrouw.'

Deborah got out of the car at once, locked it and put the keys in her handbag. She would have to get them to Gerard somehow; she had no intention of driving through Amsterdam in the BMW—getting to the hospital had been bad enough. She shuddered and followed the Sister to the lift.

They got out on the Medical floor and she was bustled through several corridors and finally through a door. 'So—we are here,' murmured the Sister, said something to whoever was in the room, gave Deborah a smile and tore away. Deborah watched her go, knowing just how she felt; probably she was saying the Dutch equivalent of 'I'll never get finished,' as she went; even the simple task of escorting someone through the hospital could make a mockery of a tight and well-planned schedule of work.

It was Doctor Schipper inside the room waiting for her. Deborah had met him before; she and Gerard had had dinner with him and his wife only the week before. She wished him a good afternoon, a little puzzled, and he came across the little room to shake her hand.

'You are surprised, Mevrouw van Doorninck, but Gerard wishes most urgently that you should have a check-up without delay. He fears that you may have strained yourself in some way—even a small cut....'

'I'm fine,' she declared, aware of sore hands. 'Well, I've broken a few fingernails and I was scared stiff!'

A young nurse had slid into the room, so Deborah, submitting to the inevitable, allowed herself

126

to be helped out of her deplorable dress and ex-amined with thoroughness by Doctor Schipper. He stood back at length. 'Quite O.K.,' he assured her. 'A rapid pulse, but I imagine you had an unpleas-ant shock—the accident was distressing. . . .'

'Yes, but I think it was having to drive the car which scared me stiff. I only drive a Fiat 500, you know—there's quite a difference. Can I go home now?'

'Of course. Nurse will arrange for you to have a taxi, but first she will clean up your hands, and perhaps an injection of A.T.S. to be on the safe side —all that earth. . . .'

She submitted to the nurse's attentions and re-membered the car keys just as she was ready to go. 'Shall I leave them at the front door?' she asked Doctor Schipper.

He held out a hand. 'Leave them with me—I'll get them to Gerard. He won't want them just yet, I imagine.'

Deborah thanked him, reminded him that he and his wife were dining with them in a few days' time and set off for the entrance with the nurse, where she climbed into a taxi and went home to find Wim and Marijke, worried about their non-appearance for lunch, waiting anxiously.

She was herself again by the evening, presenting a bandbox freshness to the world marred only by her deplorable nails and an odd bruise or two. She had deliberately put on a softly clinging dress and used her perfume with discreet lavishness; studying herself in the mirror, she decided that despite her height and curves, she looked almost fragile. She patted a stray wisp of hair into position, and much comforted by the thought, went downstairs to wait for Gerard.

He came just before dinner, gave her a brief greeting and went on: 'Well, we've saved the legs and I've done what I could with the pelvis—he's in a double hip spica.' He poured their drinks and handed hers, at the same time looking her over with what she could only describe to herself as a professional eye. 'Schipper told me that you were none the worse—you've recovered very well. Thank heaven you were with me!'

'Yes,' she spoke lightly without looking at him. 'There's nothing like beef and brawn....'

His eyes strayed over her, slowly this time and to her satisfaction, not in the least professionally. 'Did I say that? I must have been mad! Anyone less like beef and brawn I have yet to see—you look charming.'

Deborah thanked him in a level voice while her heart bounced happily. When he asked to see her hands she came and stood before him, holding them out. There were some scratches and the bruises on her knuckles were beginning to show, and the nails made her shudder. He put his drink down and stood up and surprised her very much by picking up first one hand and then the other and kissing them, and then, as if that wasn't enough, he bent his head and kissed her cheek too.

CHAPTER SEVEN

DEBORAH had gone to sleep that night in a state of mind very far removed from her usual matter-of-factness. She wakened after hours of dreaming, shreds and tatters with no beginning and no end and

128

went downstairs with the remnants of those same dreams still in her eyes. Nothing could have brought her down to earth more quickly than Gerard's brief good morning before he plunged into a list of things he begged her, if she had time, to do for him during the day—small errands which she knew quite well he would have no time to see to for himself, but it made her feel like a secretary, and from his businesslike manner he must think of her as that, or was he letting her know that his behaviour on the previous evening was a momentary weakness, not to be taken as a precedent for the future?

She went round to see her mother-in-law in the afternoon. The morning had been nicely filled with Gerard's commissions and a lesson with the professor, and now, burdened with her homework, she made her way to Mevrouw van Doorninck's flat, walking briskly because the weather, although fine, was decidedly chilly. She paused to look at one or two shops as she went; the two-piece she had worn the day before was a write-off; the earth had been ground into its fine fabric and when she had shown it to Marijke that good soul had given her opinion, with the aid of Wim, that no dry-cleaner would touch it. She would have to buy another outfit to replace it, Deborah decided, and rang the bell.

Mevrouw van Doorninck was pleased to see her. They got on very well, for the older woman had accepted her as a member of the family although she had never invited Deborah's confidence. She was urged to sit down now and tell all that had happened on the previous day.

'I didn't know you knew about it,' observed Deborah as she accepted a cup of tea.

'Gerard telephoned me in the evening—he was

so proud of you.'

Deborah managed to laugh. 'Was he? I only know that he thanked heaven that I was a strong young woman and not a—a delicate feminine creature.'

She turned her head away as she spoke; it was amazing how that still hurt. Her mother-in-law's reply was vigorous. 'You may not be delicate, my dear, but you are certainly very feminine. I can't imagine Gerard falling in love with any other type of woman.'

Deborah drank some tea. 'What about Sasja?' she asked boldly. 'Gerard told me a little about her, but what was she really like—he said that she was very pretty.'

'Very pretty—like a doll, she was also a heartless and immoral young woman and wildly extravagant. She made life for Gerard quite unbearable. And don't think, my dear,' she went on dryly, 'that I tried to interfere or influence Gerard in any way, although I longed to do so. I had to stand aside and watch Gerard make the terrible mistake of marrying her. Infatuation is far worse than love, Deborah, it blinds one to reality; it destroys ... fortunately he had his work.' She sighed. 'It is a pity that work has become such a habit with him that he hardly knows how to enjoy life any more.' She looked at Deborah, who stared back with no expression at all. 'You have found that, perhaps?'

'I know he's very busy getting everything just as he wants it at the Grotehof—I daresay when he is satisfied he'll have more time to spare.'

'Yes, dear.' Mevrouw van Doorninck's voice had that same dryness again, and Deborah wondered uneasily if she had guessed about Gerard and herself. It would be unlikely, for he always behaved beautifully towards her when there were guests or family present—he always behaved beautifully, she amended, even when they were alone. Her mother-in-law nodded. 'I'm sure you are right, my dear. Tell me, who is coming to the dinner party tomorrow evening?'

Deborah recited the names. She had met most of the guests already, there were one or two, visiting specialists, whose acquaintance she had yet to make; one of them would be spending the night. She told her mother-in-law what she intended wearing and got up to go. When she bent to kiss the older lady's cheek she was surprised at the warmth of the kiss she received in return and still more surprised when she said: 'If ever you need help or advice, Deborah, and once or twice I have thought ... no matter. If you do, come to me and I will try and help you.'

Deborah stammered her thanks and beat a hasty retreat, wondering just what Gerard's mother had meant.

She dressed early for the dinner party because she wanted to go downstairs and make sure that the table was just so, the flowers as they should be and the lamps lighted. It was to be rather a grand occasion this time because the Medical Director of the hospital was coming as well as the *Burgemeester* of the city, who, she was given to understand, was a very important person indeed. She was wearing a new dress for the occasion, a soft lavender chiffon with long full sleeves, tight cuffed with a plunging neckline discreetly veiled by pleated frills. There was a frill round the hem of the skirt too and a swathed belt which made the most of her waist. She had added the pearls and the earrings and hoped that she looked just as a successful consultant's wife should look.

'Neat but not gaudy,' she told herself aloud, inspecting her person in the big mirror on the landing, not because she hadn't seen it already in her room where there were mirrors enough, but because this particular mirror, with its elaborate gilded frame somehow enhanced her appearance.

'That's a decidedly misleading statement.' Gerard's voice came from the head of the stairs and she whirled round in a cloud of chiffon to face him.

'You're early, how nice! Everything's ready for you—I'm going down to see about the table.'

'This first.' He held out a large old-fashioned plush casket. 'You told me the colour of your dress and it seemed to me that Great-aunt Emmiline's garnets might be just the thing to go with it.'

Deborah sat down on the top tread of the staircase, her skirts billowing around her, and opened the box. Great-aunt Emmiline must have liked garnets very much; there were rings and brooches and two heavy gold bracelets set with large stones, earrings and a thick gold necklace with garnets set in it.

'They're lovely—may I really borrow them? I'll take great care. . . .'

He had come to sit beside her. 'They're yours, Deborah. I've just given them to you. I imagine you can't wear the whole lot at once, but there must be something there you like?'

'Oh, yes—yes. Thank you, Gerard, you give me so much.' She smiled at him shyly and picked out one of the bracelets and fastened it round a wrist. It looked just right; she added the necklace, putting the precious pearls in her lap. She wasn't going to take off her engagement ring; she added two of the simpler rings to the other hand and found a pair of drop earrings. She added her pearl earrings to the necklace in her lap and hooked in the garnets instead and went to look in the mirror. Gerard was right, they were exactly right with the dress. 'Have I got too much on?' she asked anxiously.

'No—just right, I should say. That's a pretty dress. What happened to the one you spoilt?'

'It's ruined. I showed it to Marijke—the stain has gone right through.'

'I'm sorry. Buy yourself another one. I'll pay for it.'

Deborah was standing with the casket clasped to her breast. 'Oh, there's no need, I've got heaps of money from my allowance.'

'Nevertheless you will allow me to pay for another dress,' he insisted blandly.

'Well—all right, thank you. I'll just put these away.'

When she came out of her room he had gone. There was nothing to do downstairs, she had seen to everything during the day and she knew that Marijke and Wim needed no prompting from her. She went and sat by the log fire Wim had lighted in the drawing room and Smith, moving with a kind of slow-motion stealth, insinuated himself on to her silken lap. But he got down again as Gerard joined them, pattering across the room when his master went to fetch the drinks and then pattering back again to arrange himself on Gerard's shoes once he had sat down. A cosy family group, thought Deborah, eyeing Gerard covertly. He looked super in a black tie—he was a man who would never lose his good looks, even when he was old. She had seen photos of his father, who in his mid-seventies had been quite something—just like his son, sitting there, stroking Smith with the toe of his shoe and talking about nothing in particular. It was a relief when the doorbell signalled the arrival of the first of their guests, because she had discovered all at once that she could not bear to sit there looking at him and loving him so much.

The evening was a success, as it could hardly have failed to have been, for Deborah had planned it carefully; the food was delicious and the guests knew and liked each other. She had felt a little flustered when the *Burgemeester* had arrived, an imposing, youngish man with a small, plump wife with no looks to speak of but with a delightful smile and a charming voice. She greeted Deborah kindly, wished her happiness upon her recent marriage and in her rather schoolgirl English wanted to know if she spoke any Dutch. It was a chance to pay tribute to the professor's teaching; Deborah made a few halting remarks, shocking as to grammar but faultless as to accent. There was a good deal of kindly laughter and when the *Burgemeester* boomed: 'Your Dutch is a delight to my ear, dear lady,' her evening was made.

She had had no time to do more than say hullo to Coenraad and Adelaide, but after dinner, with the company sitting around the drawing room, the two girls managed to get ten minutes together.

'Very nice,' said Adelaide at once, 'I can see that you're going to be a wonderful wife for Gerard—it's a great drawback to a successful man if he hasn't got a wife to see to the social side. When I first married I thought it all rather a waste of time, but I was wrong. They talk shop—oh, very discreetly, but they do—and arrange visits to seminars and who shall play host when so-and-so comes, and they ask each other's advice.... I like your dress, and the garnets are just the thing for it—another van Doorninck heirloom, I expect? I've got some too, only I have to be careful—my hair, you know.' She grinned engagingly. 'Did you go to Friesland?'

Deborah nodded. 'Yes, I loved the house, we had lunch there and then we went to see Dominic and Abigail. It's lovely there by the lake.'

'And what's all this about an accident? The hospital was positively humming with it. Coenraad told me about it, but you know what men are.'

They spent five minutes more together before Deborah, with a promise to telephone Adelaide in a few days, moved across the room to engage her mother-in-law in conversation.

It was after everyone had gone, and Doctor de Joufferie, their guest for the night, had retired to his room, that Gerard, on his way to let Smith out into the garden, told her that Claude was back in Amsterdam after a visit to Nice. 'I hear he's sold his house here and intends to live in France permanently.'

'Oh.' She paused uncertainly on her way to bed. 'He won't come here?'

'Most unlikely—if he does, would you mind?'

Deborah shook her head. 'Not in the least,' she assured her husband stoutly, minding very much.

Her answer was what he had expected, for he remarked casually 'No, you're far too sensible for that and I have no doubt that you would deal with him should he have the temerity to call.' He turned away. 'That's a pretty dress,' he told her for

135

the second time that evening.

She thanked him nicely, wishing that he had thought her pretty enough to remark upon that too; apparently he was satisfied enough that she was sensible.

She ruminated so deeply upon this unsatisfactory state of affairs that she hardly heard his thanks for the success of the evening, but she heard him out, murmured something inaudible about being tired, and went to bed.

Doctor de Joufferie joined them for breakfast in the morning, speaking an English almost as perfect as Gerard's. The two men spent most of the time discussing the possibility of Gerard going to Paris for some conference or other: 'And I hope very much that you will accompany your husband,' their visitor interrupted himself to say. 'My wife would be delighted to show you a little of Paris while we are at the various sessions.'

Deborah gave him a vague, gracious answer; she didn't want to hurt the doctor's feelings, but on the other hand she wasn't sure whether Gerard would want her to go with him; he had never suggested, even remotely, such a possibility. She led the conversation carefully back to the safe ground of Paris and its delights, at the same time glancing at her husband to see how he was reacting. He wasn't, his expression was politely attentive and nothing more, but then it nearly always was; even if he had no wish to take her, he would never dream of saying so.

The two men left together and she accompanied them to the door, to be pleasantly surprised at the admiration in the Frenchman's eyes as he kissed her hand with the hope that they might meet again soon. She glowed pleasantly under his look, but the glow was damped immediately by Gerard's brief, cool kiss which just brushed her cheek.

She spent an hour or so pottering round the house, getting in Wim's way, and then went to sit with her Dutch lesson, but she was in no mood to learn. She flung the books pettishly from her and went out. Gerard had told her to buy a new dress—all right, so she would, and take good care not to look too closely at the price tag. She walked along the Keizersgracht until she came to that emporium of high fashion, Metz, and once inside, buoyed up by strong feelings which she didn't bother to define, she went straight to the couture department. She had in mind another tweed outfit, or perhaps one of the thicker jersey suits. She examined one or two, a little shocked at their prices, although even after so short a time married to Gerard, she found that her shock was lessening.

It was while she was prowling through the thickly carpeted alcove which held the cream of the Autumn collection that she saw the dress—a Gina Fratini model for the evening—white silk, high-necked and long-sleeved, pin-tucked and gathered and edged with antique lace. Deborah examined it more closely; it wouldn't be her size, of course, and even if it were, when would she wear it, and what astronomical price would it be? She circled round it once more; it would do very well for the big ball Gerard had casually mentioned would take place at the hospital before Christmas, and what about the *Burgemeester's* reception? But the size? The saleswoman, who had been hovering discreetly, pounced delicately. She even remembered Deborah's name, so that she felt like an old and valued customer, and what was more, her English was good.

'A lovely gown, Mevrouw van Doorninck,' she said persuasively, 'and so right for you, and I fancy it is your size.' She had it over her arm now, yards and yards of soft silk. 'Would you care to try it on?'

'Well,' said Deborah weakly, 'I really came in for something in tweed or jersey.' She caught the woman's eye and smiled. 'Yes, I'll try it on.'

It was a perfect fit and utterly lovely. She didn't need the saleswoman's flattering remarks to know it. The dress did something for her, although she wasn't sure what. She said quickly, before she should change her mind: 'I'll take it—will you charge it to my husband, please?'

It was when she was dressed again, watching it being lovingly packed, that she asked the price. She had expected it to be expensive, but the figure the saleswoman mentioned so casually almost took her breath. Deborah waited for a feeling of guilt to creep over her, and felt nothing; Gerard had insisted on paying for a dress, hadn't he? Declining an offer to have it delivered, she carried her precious box home.

She would have tried it on then and there, but Wim met her in the hall with the news that Marijke had a delicious soufflé only waiting to be eaten within a few minutes. But eating lunch by herself was something quickly done with, so she flew upstairs to her room and unpacked the dress. It looked even more super than it had done in the shop. She put it on and went to turn and twist before the great mirror—she had put on the pearls and the earrings and a pair of satin slippers; excepting for the faint untidiness of the heavy chignon, she looked ready for a ball.

'Cinderella, and more beautiful than ever,' said Claude from the stairs.

Deborah turned round slowly, not quite believing that he was there, but he was, smiling and debonair, for all the world as though Gerard had never told him not to enter the house again.

'What are you doing here?' she asked, and tried to keep the angry shake from her voice.

'Why, come to pay you a farewell visit. I'm leaving this city, thank heaven, surely you've heard that? But I couldn't go until I had said goodbye to you, but don't worry, I telephoned the hospital and they told me that Gerard was busy, so I knew that it was safe to come, and very glad I am that I did. A ball so early in the day? Or is the boy-friend coming?'

Her hand itched to slap his smiling face. 'How silly you are,' she remarked scathingly. 'And you have no right to walk into the house as though it were your own. Why didn't you ring the bell?'

'Ah, I came in through the little door in the garden. You forget, my lovely Deborah, that I have known this house since many years; many a time I've used that door.' He was lounging against the wall, laughing at her, so that her carefully held patience deserted her.

'Well, you can go, and out of the front door this time. I've nothing to say to you, and I'm sure Gerard would be furious if he knew that you had come here.'

He snapped his fingers airily. 'My dear good girl, let us be honest, you have no idea whether Gerard would be annoyed or not; you have no idea about anything he does or thinks or plans, have you? I don't suppose he tells you anything. Shall I tell you what I think? Why, that you're a figurehead to adorn his table, a hostess for his guests and a competent housekeeper to look after his home while he's away—and where does he go, I wonder? Have you ever wondered? Hours in the Grotehof—little trips to Paris, Brussels, Vienna, operating here, lecturing there while you sit at home thinking what thoughts?'

He stopped speaking and stared at her pinched face. 'I'm right, aren't I? I have hit the nail on its English head, have I not? Poor beautiful Deborah.' He laughed softly and came closer. 'Leave him, my lovely, and come to Nice with me—why not? We could have a good time together.'

She wasn't prepared for his sudden swoop; she was a strong girl, but he had hold of her tightly, and besides, at the back of her stunned mind was the thought that if she struggled too much her beautiful dress would be ruined. She turned her face away as he bent to kiss her and brought up a hand to box him soundly on the ear. But he laughed the more as she strained away from him, her head drawn back. So that she didn't see or hear Gerard coming up the stairs, although Claude did. She felt his hold tighten as he spoke.

'Gerard—hullo, *jongen*, I knew you wouldn't mind me calling in to say goodbye to Deborah, and bless her heart, she wouldn't let me go without one last kiss.'

She felt him plucked from her, heard, as in a dream, his apology, no doubt induced by the painful grip Gerard had upon him, and watched in a detached way as he was marched down the stairs across the hall to disappear in the direction of the front door, which presently shut with some force. Gerard wasn't even breathing rapidly when he rejoined her, only his eyes blazed in his set face.

'You knew he was coming?' His tone was conversational but icy.

'Of course not.' She was furious to find that she was trembling.

'How did he get in? Doesn't Wim open the door?'

'Of course he does—when the bell rings. He—he came in through the door in the garden. I had no idea that he was in the house until he spoke to me here.' She essayed a smile which wavered a little. 'I'm glad you came home.'

'Yes?' His eyebrows rose in faint mockery. 'You didn't appear to be resisting Claude with any great show of determination.'

She fired up at that. 'He took me by surprise. I slapped his cheek.'

'Did you call Wim?'

Deborah shook her head. Truth to tell, it hadn't entered her head.

Her husband stared at her thoughtfully. 'A great strapping girl like you,' he commented nastily. 'No kicking? No struggling?'

She hated him, mostly because he had called her a strapping girl. She wanted to cry too, but the tears were in a hard knot in her chest. She said sullenly: 'I was trying on this dress—it's new....' He laughed then and she said desperately: 'You don't believe me, do you? You actually think that I would encourage him.' Her voice rose with the strength of her feelings. 'Well, if that's what you want to believe, you may do so!'

She swept to her bedroom door and remembered

something as she reached it. 'I bought this dress because you told me to and I've charged it to you—it's a model and it cost over a thousand gulden, and I'm glad!' She stamped her foot. 'I wish it had cost twice as much!'

She banged the door behind her and locked it, which was a silly action anyway, for when had he ever tried the door handle?

She took the dress off carefully and hung it away and put on a sober grey dress, then combed her hair and put on too much lipstick and went downstairs. She was crossing the hall when Gerard opened his study door and invited her to join him in a quiet voice which she felt would be wiser to obey. She went past him with her head in the air and didn't sit down when he asked her to.

'I came home to pack a bag,' he told her mildly, all trace of ill-humour vanished. 'There is an urgent case I have to see in Geneva and probably operate on. I intend to catch the five o'clock flight and I daresay I shall be away for two days. I'm sorry to spring it on you like this, but there's nothing important for a few days, is there?'

'Nothing.' Wild horses wouldn't have dragged from her the information that it was her birthday in two days' time. She had never mentioned it to him and he had never tried to find out.

He nodded. 'Good——' he broke off as Wim came in with a sheaf of flowers which he gave to Deborah. 'Just delivered, Mevrouw,' he told her happily, and went away, leaving a heavy silence behind him.

Deborah started to open the envelope pinned to its elaborate wrapping and then stopped; supposing it was from Claude? It was the sort of diabolical

142

joke he would dream up....

She looked up and found Gerard watching her with a speculative eye and picked up the flowers and walked to the door. 'I'll pack you a case,' she told him. 'Will you want a black tie, or is it to be strictly work?'

His eyes narrowed. 'Oh, strictly work,' he assured her in a silky voice, 'and even if it weren't, a black tie isn't always essential in order to—er—enjoy yourself.'

He gave her a look of such mockery that she winced under it; it was almost as if Claude's poisoned remarks held a grain of truth.

Outside she tore open the little envelope and read the card; the flowers were from Doctor Joufferie. She suppressed her strong desire to run straight back to Gerard and show it to him, and went to pack his bag instead.

It was quiet in the house after he had gone. Deborah spent the long evening working at her Dutch, playing with Smith and leafing through magazines, and went to bed at last with a bad headache. She had expected Gerard to telephone, but he didn't, which made the headache worse. There was no call in the morning either; she hung around until lunchtime and then went out with Smith trotting beside her on his lead. She walked for a long time, and it was on her way back, close to the house, that she stopped to pick up a very small child who had fallen over, the last in a line of equally small uniformed children, walking ahead of her. She had seen them before, and supposed that they went to some nursery school or other in one of the narrow streets leading from the Keizersgracht. She comforted the little girl, mopped up a

143

grazed knee and carried her towards the straggling line of her companions. She had almost reached it when a nun darted back towards them, breaking into voluble Dutch as she did so.

Deborah stood still. 'So sorry,' she managed, 'my Dutch is bad.'

The nun smiled. 'Then I will speak my bad English to you. Thank you for helping the little one—there are so many of them and my companion has gone on to the Weeshuis with a message.'

Deborah glanced across the road to where an old building stood under the shadow of the great Catholic church. 'Oh,' she said, and remembered that a Weeshuis was an orphanage. 'They're little orphans.'

The nun smiled again. 'Yes. We have many of them. The older ones go to school, but these are still too small. We go now to play and sing a little after their walk. Once we had a lady who came each week and told them stories and played games with them. They liked that.' She held out her arms for the child and said: 'I thank you again, Mevrouw,' and walked rapidly away to where the obedient line of children waited. Deborah watched them disappear inside the orphanage before she went home.

It was after her lonely tea that she had an idea. Without pausing to change her mind, she left the house and went back to the orphanage and rang the bell, and when an old nun came to peer at her through the grille, she asked to see the Mother Superior. Half an hour later she was back home again after an interview with that rather surprised lady; she might go once a week and play with the children until such time as a permanent helper could be found. She had pointed out hesitantly that she wasn't a Catholic herself, but the Mother Superior didn't seem to mind. Thursday evenings, she had suggested, and any time Deborah found the little orphans too much for her, she had only to say so.

The morning post brought a number of cards and parcels for her. She read them while she ate her breakfast and was just getting up from the table when Wim came in with a great bouquet of flowers and a gaily tied box.

'Mijnheer told me to give you these, Mevrouw,' he informed her in a fatherly fashion, 'and Marijke and I wish you a very happy birthday.' He produced a small parcel with the air of a magician and she opened it at once. Handkerchiefs, dainty, lace-trimmed ones. She thanked him nicely, promised that she would go to the kitchen within a few minutes so that she could thank Marijke, and was left to examine her flowers. They were exquisite; roses and carnations and sweet peas and lilies, out of season and delicate and fragrant. She sniffed at them with pleasure and read the card which accompanied them. It bore the austere message: With best wishes, G. So he had known all the time! She opened the box slowly; it contained a set of dressing table silver, elegantly plain with her initials on each piece surmounted by the family crest. There was another card too, less austere than its fellow. This one said: 'To Deborah, wishing you a happy birthday.'

She went upstairs and arranged the silver on her dressing table, and stood admiring it until she remembered that she had to see Marijke. She spent a long time arranging the flowers so that she was a little late for her lesson and Professor de Wit was a little put out, but she had learnt her lesson well, which mollified him sufficiently for him to offer her a cup of coffee when they had finished wrestling with the Dutch verbs for the day. She went back home presently to push the food around her plate and then go upstairs to her room. Her mother-in-law was in Hilversum, she could hardly telephone Adelaide and tell her that it was her birthday and she was utterly miserable. Thank heaven it was Thursday; at least she had her visit to the orphans to look forward to.

There was still no word from Gerard. Deborah told Wim that she was going for a walk and would be back for dinner at half past seven as usual, and set out. The evenings were chilly now and the streets were crowded with people on their way home or going out to enjoy themselves, but the narrow street where the orphanage was was quiet as she rang the bell.

The orphans assembled for their weekly junketings in a large, empty room overlooking the street, reached through a long narrow passage and a flight of steps, and one of the dreariest rooms Deborah had ever seen, but there was a piano and plenty of room for twenty-eight small children. It was when she had thrown off her coat and turned to survey them that she remembered that her Dutch was, to say the least, very indifferent. But she had reckoned without the children; within five minutes they had discovered the delights of 'Hunt the Slipper' and were screaming their heads off.

At the end of the hour they had mastered Grandmother's Steps too as well as Twos and Threes, and for the last ten minutes or so, in order

that they might calm down a little, she began to
tell them a story, mostly in English of course, with
a few Dutch words thrown in here and there and a
great deal of mime. It seemed to go down very well,
as did the toffees Deborah produced just before the
nun came to fetch them away to their supper and
bed. An hour had never gone so quickly. She kissed
them good night, one by one, and when they had
gone the empty room seemed emptier and drearier
than ever. She tidied it up quickly and went home.

Indoors, it was to hear from Wim that Gerard
had telephoned, but only to leave a message that he
would be home the following evening. Deborah
thanked him and went to eat her dinner, choking it
down as best she could because Marijke had
thought up a splendid one for her birthday. Afterwards, with Smith on her lap, she watched T.V. It
was a film she had already seen several times in
England, but she watched it to its end before going
to bed.

Gerard came home late the following afternoon.
Deborah had spent the day wondering how to greet
him. As though nothing had happened? With an
apology? She ruled this one out, for she had nothing to apologize for—with a dignified statement
pointing out how unfair he had been? She was still
rehearsing a variety of opening speeches when she
heard his key in the door.

There was no need for her to make a speech of
any kind; it riled her to find that his manner was
exactly as it always was, quiet, pleasant—he was
even smiling. Taken aback, Deborah replied to his
cheerful hullo with a rather uncertain one followed by the hope that he had had a good trip and
that everything had been successful. And would he

like something to eat?

He declined her offer on his way to the door. 'I've some telephoning to do,' he told her. 'The post is in the study, I suppose?'

She said that yes, it was and as he reached the door, said in a rush: 'Thank you for the lovely flowers and your present—it's quite super—I didn't know that you knew....'

'Our marriage certificate,' he pointed out briefly. 'I'm sorry I was not here to celebrate it in the usual Dutch manner—another year, perhaps.'

'No, well—it didn't matter. It's a marvellous present.'

Gerard was almost through the door. He paused long enough to remark:

'I'm glad you like it. It seemed to me to be a suitable gift.' He didn't look at her and his voice sounded cold. He closed the door very quietly behind him.

Deborah threw a cushion at it. 'I hate him,' she raged, 'hate him! He's pompous and cold and he doesn't care a cent for me, not one cent—a suitable present indeed! And just what was he doing in Geneva?' she demanded of the room at large. She plucked a slightly outraged Smith from the floor and hugged him to her. 'None of that's true,' she assured him fiercely, and opened the door and let him into the hall. She heard him scratching on the study door and after a few moments it was opened for him.

They dined together later, apparently on the best of terms; Deborah told Gerard one or two items which she thought might interest him, but never a word about the orphans, The van Doornincks were Calvinists; several ancestors had been

148

put to death rather nastily by the Spaniards during their occupation of the Netherlands. It was a very long time ago, but the Dutch had long memories for such things. She didn't think that Gerard would approve of her helping, even for an hour, in a convent. Her conscience pricked her a little because she was being disloyal to him; on the other hand, she wasn't a Catholic either, but that hadn't made any difference to her wish to help the children in some small way. She put the matter out of her mind and asked him as casually as possible about his trip to Geneva.

She might have saved her breath, for although he talked about Switzerland and Geneva in particular, not one crumb of information as to his activities while he was there did he offer her. She rose from the table feeling frustrated and ill-tempered and spent the rest of the evening sitting opposite him in the sitting room, doing her embroidery all wrong. Just the same, when she went to bed she said quite humbly: 'I'm really very sorry to have bought such an expensive dress, Gerard—I'll pay you back out of my next quarter's allowance.'

'I offered you a new dress,' he reminded her suavely. 'I don't remember telling you to buy the cheapest one you saw. Shall we say no more about it?'

Upon which unsatisfactory remark she went to bed.

It didn't seem possible that they could go on as before, with no mention of Claude, no coolness between them, no avoiding of each other's company, but it was. Deborah found that life went on exactly as before, with occasional dinner parties, drinks with friends, visits to her mother-in-law and Gerard's family and an occasional quiet evening at home with Gerard—and of course the weekly visit to the orphans.

It was getting colder now, although the autumn had stretched itself almost into winter with its warm days and blue skies. But now the trees by the canal were without leaves and the water looked lifeless; it was surprising what a week or so would do at that time of year, and that particular evening, coming home from the convent, there was an edge of winter in the air.

Deborah found Gerard at home. He was always late on Thursdays and when she walked into the sitting room and found him there she was surprised into saying so.

'I've been out,' she explained a little inadequately. 'It was such a nice evening,' and then could have bitten out her tongue, for there was a nasty wind blowing and the beginnings of a fine, cold rain. She put a guilty hand up to her hair and felt its dampness.

'I'll tell Marijke to serve dinner at once,' she told him, 'and change my dress.'

That had been a silly thing to say too, for the jersey suit she was wearing was decidedly crumpled from the many small hands which had clung to it. But Gerard said nothing and if his hooded eyes noticed anything, they gave nothing away. She joined him again presently and spent the evening waiting for him to ask her where she had been, and when he didn't, went to bed in a fine state of nervous tension.

Several days later he told her that he would be going away again for a day and possibly the night as well.

'Not Geneva?' asked Deborah, too quickly.

He was in the garden, brushing Smith. 'No—Arnhem.'

'But Arnhem is only a short distance away,' she pointed out, 'surely you could come home?'

He raised his eyes to hers. 'If I should come home, it would be after ten o'clock,' he told her suavely. 'That is a certainty, so that you can safely make any plans you wish for the evening.'

She stared at him, puzzled. 'But I haven't any plans—where should I want to go?'

He shrugged. 'Where do you go on Thursday evenings?' he asked blandly, and when she hesitated, 'That was unfair of me—I'm sorry. I only learned of it through overhearing something Wim said. Perhaps you would rather not tell me.'

'No—that is, no,' she answered miserably. 'I don't think so.'

Gerard flashed her a quizzical glance. 'Quid pro quo?' he asked softly.

She flushed and lifted her chin. 'When I married you, you made it very clear what you expected of me. Maybe I've fallen short of—of your expectations, but I have done my best, but I wouldn't stoop to paying you back in your own coin!'

She flounced out of the room before he could speak and went to her room and banged the door. They were going out that evening to dinner with a colleague of Gerard's. She came downstairs at exactly the moment when it was necessary to leave the house, looking quite magnificent in the pink silk jersey dress and the pearls and with such a haughty expression upon her lovely face that Gerard, after the briefest of glances, forbore from speaking. When she peeped at him his face was impassive, but she had the ridiculous feeling that he was laughing at her.

He had left the house when she got down in the morning. She had breakfast, did a few chores around the house and prepared to go out. She was actually at the front door when the telephone rang and when she answered it, it was to hear Sien's voice, a little agitated, asking for Gerard.

'Wim,' called Deborah urgently, and made placating noises to Sien, and when he came: 'It's Sien —I can't understand her very well, but I think there's something wrong.'

Sien had cut her hand, Wim translated, and it was the local doctor's day off and no one near enough to help; the season was over, the houses, and they were only a few, within reach were closed for the winter. She had tied her hand up, but it had bled a great deal. Perhaps she needed stitches? and would Mevrouw forgive her for telephoning, but she wasn't sure what she should do.

'Ask her where the cut is,' commanded Deborah, 'and if it's still bleeding.' And when Wim had told her, gave careful instructions: 'And tell her to sit down and try and keep her arm up, and that I'm on my way now—I'll be with her in less than two hours.'

She was already crossing the hall to Gerard's study where she knew there was a well-stocked cupboard of all she might require. She chose what she needed and went to the front door. 'I don't know how long I shall be, Wim,' she said. 'You'd better keep Smith here. I expect I may have to take Sien to hospital for some stitches and then try and find someone who would stay a day or two with her —she can't be alone.'

'Very good, Mevrouw,' said Wim in his fatherly fashion, 'and I beg you to be careful on the road.'

She smiled at him—he was such an old dear. 'Of course, Wim, I'll be home later.'

'And if the master should come home?'

Deborah didn't look at him. 'He said after ten this evening, or even tomorrow, Wim.'

She drove the Fiat fast and without any hold-ups, for the tourists had gone and the roads were fairly empty; as she slowed to turn into the little lane leading to the house she thought how lovely it looked against the pale sky and the wide country around it, but she didn't waste time looking around her; she parked the car and ran inside.

Sien had done exactly as she had been told. She looked a little pale and the rough bandage was heavily bloodstained, but she greeted Deborah cheerfully and submitted to having the cut examined.

'A stitch or two,' explained Deborah in her threadbare Dutch, knowing that it would need far more than that, for the cut was deep and long, across the palm.

'Coffee,' she said hearteningly, and made it for both of them, then helped Sien to put on her coat and best hat—for was she not going to hospital to see a doctor, she wanted to know when Deborah brought the wrong one—locked the door and settled her companion in the little car. It wasn't far to Leeuwarden and Sien knew where the hospital was.

She hadn't known that Gerard was known there too. She only had to give her name and admit to being his wife for Sien to be given V.I.P. treatment. She was stitched, given A.T.S., told when to

153

come again and given another cup of coffee while Deborah had a little talk with the Casualty Officer.

'Can I help you at all?' he wanted to know as he handed her coffee too.

She explained thankfully about Sien being alone. 'If someone could find out if she has a friend or family nearby who would go back with her for a day or two, I could collect them on the way back. If not, I think I should take her back with me to Amsterdam or stay here myself.'

She waited patiently while Sien was questioned. 'There's a niece,' the young doctor told her, 'she lives at Warga, quite close to your house. Your housekeeper says that she will be pleased to stay with her for a few days.'

'You're very kind,' said Deborah gratefully. 'It's a great hindrance not being able to speak the language, you know. My husband will be very grateful when he hears how helpful you have been.'

The young man went a dusky red. 'Your husband is a great surgeon, Mevrouw. We would all wish to be like him.'

She shook hands. 'I expect you will be,' she assured him, and was rewarded by his delighted smile.

Sien's niece was a young edition of her aunt, just as tall and plump and just as sensible. Deborah drove the two of them back to the house, gave instructions that they were to telephone the house at Amsterdam if they were in doubt about anything, asked them if they had money enough, made sure that Sien understood about the pills she was to take if her hand got too painful, wished them goodbye, and got into the Fiat again. It was early afternoon, she would be home for tea.

CHAPTER EIGHT

But she wasn't home for tea; it began to rain as she reached the outskirts of the city, picking her careful way through streets which became progressively narrower and busier as she neared the heart of the city. The cobbles glistened in the rain, their surface made treacherous; Deborah had no chance at all when a heavy lorry skidded across the street, sweeping her little car along with it. By some miracle the Fiat stayed upright despite the ominous crunching noises it was making. Indeed, its bonnet was a shapeless mass by the time the lorry came to a precarious halt with Deborah's car inextricably welded to it.

She climbed out at once, white and shaking but quite unhurt except for one or two sharp knocks. The driver of the lorry got out too to engage her immediately in earnest conversation, not one word of which did she understand. Dutch, she had discovered long since, wasn't too bad provided one had the time and the circumstances were favourable. They were, at the moment, very unfavourable. She looked round helplessly, not at all sure what to do—there were a dozen or more people milling about them, all seemingly proffering advice.

'Can't anyone speak English?' she asked her growing audience. Apparently not; there was a short pause before they all burst out again, even more eager to help. It was a relief when Deborah glimpsed the top of a policeman's cap above the heads, forging its way with steady authority towards her. Presently he came into full view, a grizzled man with a harsh face. Her heart sank; awful visions of spending the night in prison and no one any the wiser were floating through her bemused brain. When he spoke to her she asked, without any hope at all: 'I suppose you don't speak English?'

He smiled and his face wasn't harsh any more. 'A little,' he admitted. 'I will speak to this man first, Mevrouw.'

The discussion was lengthy with a good deal of argument. When at length the police officer turned to her she hastened to tell him:

'It wasn't anyone's fault—the road was slippery —he skidded, he wasn't driving fast at all.'

The man answered in a laboured English which was more than adequate. 'He tells me that also, Mevrouw. You have your papers?'

She managed to open the car's battered door and took them out of her handbag. He examined her licence and then looked at her. 'You are wife of Mijnheer Doorninck, *chirurg* at the Grotehof hospital.'

She nodded.

'You are not injured, Mevrouw?'

'I don't think so—I feel a little shaky.' She smiled. 'I was scared stiff!'

'Stiff?' He eyed her anxiously.

'Sorry—I was frightened.'

'I shall take you to the hospital in one moment.' He was writing in his notebook. 'You will sit in your car, please.'

Deborah did as she was told and he went back to talk some more to the lorry driver, who presently got into his cab and drove away.

'It will be arranged that your car'—his eye swept

over the poor remnant of it—'will be taken to a garage. Do not concern yourself about it, Mevrouw. Now you will come with me, please.'

'I'm quite all right,' she assured him, and then at his look, followed him obediently to the police car behind the crowd, glad to sit down now, for her legs were suddenly jelly and one arm was aching.

They were close to the hospital. She was whisked there, swept from the car and ushered into the Accident Room where Gerard's name acted like a magic wand; she barely had time to thank the policeman warmly before she was spirited away to be meticulously examined from head to foot. There was nothing wrong, the Casualty Officer decided, save for a few painful bruises on her arm and the nasty shock she had had.

'I will telephone and inform Mijnheer van Doorninck,' he told her, and she stifled a giggle, for Gerard's name had been uttered with such reverence. 'He's not home,' she told him, 'not until late this evening or tomorrow morning—he's in Arnhem. In any case, I'm perfectly all right.'

She should have suspected him when he agreed with her so readily, suggesting that she should drink a cup of tea and have a short rest, then he would come back and pronounce her fit to go home.

She drank the tea gratefully. There was no milk with it, but it was hot and sweet and it pulled her together and calmed her down. She lay back and closed her eyes and wondered what Gerard would say when he got back. She was asleep in five minutes.

She slept for just over an hour and when she wakened Gerard was there, staring down at her, his blue eyes blazing from a white face. She wondered, only half awake, why he looked so furiously angry, and then remembered where she was.

She exclaimed unhappily: 'Oh, dear—were you home after all? But I did tell them not to telephone the house....'

'I was telephoned at Arnhem. How do you feel?'

Deborah ignored that. 'The fools,' she said crossly, 'I told them you were busy, that there was no need to bother you.'

'They quite rightly ignored such a foolish remark. How do you feel?' he repeated.

She swung her legs off the couch to let him see just how normal she was. 'Perfectly all right, thank you—such a fuss about nothing.' She gulped suddenly. 'I'm so sorry, Gerard, I've made you angry, haven't I? You didn't have to give up the case or anything awful like that?'

His grim mouth relaxed into the faintest of smiles. 'No—I had intended returning home this evening, anyway. And I am not angry.'

She eyed him uncertainly. 'You look....' She wasn't sure how he looked; probably he was tired after a long-drawn-out operation. She forced her voice to calm. 'I'm perfectly able to go home now, Gerard, if that's convenient for you.'

He said slowly, studying his hands: 'Is that how you think of me? As someone whose wishes come before everything else? Who doesn't give a damn when his wife is almost killed—a heartless tyrant?'

She was sitting on the side of the couch, conscious that her hair was an untidy mop halfway down her neck and that she had lost the heel of a shoe and her stockings were laddered. 'You're not a heartless tyrant,' she protested hotly. 'You're not—

you're a kind and considerate husband. Can't you see that's why I hate to hinder you in any way? It's the least I can do—I'd rather die....'

She had said too much, she realized that too late.

'Just what do you mean by that?' he asked her sharply.

Deborah opened her mouth, not having any idea what to say and was saved from making matters worse by the entry of the Casualty Officer, eager to know if she felt up to going home and obviously pleased with himself because he had come under the notice of one of the most eminent consultants in the hospital and treated his wife to boot. He was a worthy young man, his thoughts were written clearly on his face, Deborah thanked him cordially and was pleased when Gerard added his own thanks with a warmth to make the young man flush with pleasure. She hadn't realized that Gerard was held in such veneration by the hospital staff; the things she didn't know about him were so many that it was a little frightening—certainly they were seen to the entrance by an imposing number of people.

The BMW was parked right in front of the steps; anyone else, she felt sure would have been ordered to move their car, for no one could get near the entrance, but no one seemed to find anything amiss. Gerard helped her in and she sat back with a sigh. As he drove through the hospital gateway she said apologetically: 'The police said they would take the Fiat away and they'd let you know about it. It—it's a bit battered.'

'It can be scrapped.' His voice was curt. 'I'll get you a new car.'

That was all he said on the way home and she

could think of nothing suitable to talk about herself. Besides, her head had begun to ache. Wim and Marijke were both hovering in the hall when they got in. Gerard said something to them in Dutch and Marijke came forward, talking volubly.

'Marijke will help you to bed,' Gerard explained. 'I suggest that you have something to eat there and then get a good sleep—you'll feel quite the thing by the morning.' His searching eyes rested for a brief, professional minute on her face. 'You have a headache, I daresay, I'll give you something for that presently. Go up to bed now.'

She would have liked to have disputed his order, but when she considered it, bed was the one place where she most wanted to be. She thanked him in a subdued voice and went upstairs, Marijke in close attendance.

She wasn't hungry, she discovered, when she was tucked up against her pillows and Marijke had brought in a tray of soup and chicken. She took a few mouthfuls, put the tray on the side table and lay back and closed her eyes, to open them at once as Gerard came in after the most perfunctory of knocks. He walked over to the bed, took her pulse, studied the bruises beginning to show on her arm, and then stood looking down at her with the expression she imagined he must wear when he was examining his patients—a kind of reserved kindliness. 'You've not eaten anything,' he observed.

'I'm not very hungry.'

He nodded, shook some pills out of the box he held, fetched water from the carafe on the table and said: 'Swallow these down—they'll take care of that headache and send you to sleep.'

She did as she was bid and lay back again against

the pillows.

'Ten minutes?' she wanted to know. 'Pills always seem to take so long to work.'

'Then we might as well talk while we're waiting,' he said easily, and sat down on the end of the bed. 'Tell me, what is all this about Sien? Wim tells me that you went up to Domwier because she had cut her hand.'

'Yes—the doctor wasn't there and it sounded as though it might have needed a stitch or two—she had six, actually. I—I thought you would want me to look after her as you weren't home.'

He took her hand lying on the coverlet and his touch was gentle. 'Yes, of course that was exactly what I should have wanted you to do, Deborah. Was it a bad cut?'

She told him; she told him about their visit to the hospital at Leeuwarden too, adding: 'They knew you quite well there—I didn't know....' There was such a lot she didn't know, she thought wearily. 'I got the doctor there to find out if Sien had any friends or family—I fetched her niece, they seemed quite happy together.' She blinked huge, drowsy eyes. 'I forgot—I said I would telephone and make sure that Sien was all right. Could someone...?'

'I'll see to it. Thank you, my dear. What a competent girl you are, but you always were in theatre and you're just as reliable now.'

She was really very sleepy, but she had to answer that. 'No, I'm not. I bought that terribly expensive dress just to annoy you—and what about Claude? Have you forgotten him? You thought I was quite unreliable with him, didn't you?'

She was aware that her tongue was running away

with her, but she seemed unable to help herself. 'Don't you know that I...?' She fell asleep, just in time.

She was perfectly all right in the morning except for a badly discoloured arm. All the same, Marijke brought her breakfast up on a tray with the injunction, given with motherly sternness, to eat it up, and she was closely followed by Gerard, who wished her a placid good morning and cast a quick eye over her. 'I've told Wim,' he said as he was leaving after the briefest of stays, 'that if anyone telephones about the Fiat that he is to refer them to me. And by the way, Sien is quite all right. I telephoned last night and again this morning. She sends her respects.'

Deborah smiled. 'How very old-fashioned that sounds, and how nice! But she's a nice person, isn't she? I can't wait to learn a little of her language so that we can really talk.'

He smiled. 'She would like that. But first your Dutch—it's coming along very nicely, Deborah—your grammar is a little wild, but your accent is impeccable.'

She flushed with pleasure. 'Oh, do you really mean that? Professor de Wit is so loath to praise. I sometimes feel that I'm making no headway at all.' She smiled at him. 'I'm glad you're pleased.'

He opened the door without answering her. 'I shouldn't do too much today,' was all he said as he went.

If he had been there for her to say it to, she would have told him that she didn't do too much anyway because there was nothing for her to do, but that would have sounded ungrateful; he had given her everything she could possibly want—a lovely home, clothes beyond her wildest dreams, a car, an allowance which she secretly felt was far too generous—all these, and none of them worth a cent without his love and interest. She had sometimes wondered idly what the term 'an empty life' had meant. Now she knew, although it wouldn't be empty if he loved her; then everything which they did would be shared—the dinner parties, the concerts, the visits to friends, just as he would share the burden of his work with her. Deborah sighed and got out of bed and went to look out of the window. It was a cold, clear morning. She got dressed and presently telephoned Adelaide van Essen and invited her round for coffee.

It was two days later that Deborah mentioned at breakfast that she had never seen Gerard's consulting rooms and, to her surprise, was invited to visit them that very day.

'I shan't be there,' he explained with his usual courtesy. 'I don't see patients there on a Thursday afternoon—it's my heavy afternoon list at the Grotehof, but go along by all means. Trudi, my secretary, will be there—her English is just about as good as your Dutch, so you should get on very well together.'

He had left soon afterwards, leaving her a prey to a variety of feelings, not the least of which was the sobering one that he had shown no visible regret at not being able to take her himself. Still, it would be something to do.

She went after lunch, in a new tweed suit because the sun was shining, albeit weakly. She was conscious that she looked rather dishy and consoled herself with the thought that at last she was being allowed to see another small, very small, facet of

Gerard's life.

The consulting rooms were within walking distance, in a quiet square lined with tall brick houses, almost all of which had brass plates on their doors—a kind of Dutch Harley Street, she gathered, and found Gerard's name quickly enough. His rooms were on the first floor and Deborah was impressed by their unobtrusive luxury; pale grey carpet, solid, comfortable chairs, small tables with flowers, and in one corner a desk where Trudi sat.

Trudi was young and pretty and dressed discreetly in grey to match the carpet. She welcomed Deborah a little nervously in an English as bad as her Dutch and showed her round, leaving Gerard's own room till last. It too was luxurious, deliberately comfortable and relaxing so that the patient might feel at ease. She smiled and nodded as Trudi rattled on, not liking to ask too many questions because, as Gerard's wife, she should already know the answers. They had a cup of tea together presently and because Trudi kept looking anxiously at the clock, Deborah got up to go. Probably the poor girl had a great deal of work to do before she could leave. She was halfway across the sea of carpet when the door opened and Claude came in. She was so surprised that she came to a halt, her mouth open, but even in her surprise she saw that he was taken aback, annoyed too. He cast a lightning glance at Trudi and then back to Deborah. 'Hullo, my beauty,' he said.

She ignored that. 'What are you doing here?' she demanded, 'I'm quite sure that Gerard doesn't know. What do you want?'

He still looked shaken, although he replied airily enough. 'Oh, nothing much. Trudi has something for me, haven't you, darling?'

The girl looked so guilty that Deborah felt sorry for her. 'Yes—yes, I have. It's downstairs, I'll get it.'

She fled through the door leaving Deborah frowning at Claude's now smiling face. 'What are you up to?' she wanted to know.

'I?' he smiled even more widely. 'My dear girl, nothing. Surely I can come and see my friends without you playing the schoolmarm over me?'

'But this is Gerard's office....'

'We do meet in the oddest places, don't we?' He came a step nearer. 'Jealous, by any chance? Gerard would never dream of looking for us here....'

'You underestimate my powers,' said Gerard in a dangerously quiet voice. 'And really, this time, Claude, my patience is exhausted.'

He had been standing in the open doorway. Now he crossed the room without haste, knocked Claude down in a businesslike fashion, picked him up again and frogmarched him out of the room. Deborah, ice-cold with the unexpectedness of it all, listened to the muddle of feet going down the stairs. It sounded as though Claude was having difficulty in keeping his balance. The front door was shut with quiet finality and Gerard came back upstairs. He looked as placid as usual and yet quite murderous.

'Is this why you wanted to visit these rooms?' he asked silkily.

She had never seen him look like that before. 'No, you know that.'

'Why is Trudi not here?'

'Trudi?' She had forgotten the girl, she hadn't the least idea where she had gone. 'She went to fetch something for Claude—he didn't say what it was.'

'She is downstairs, very upset,' he informed her coldly. 'She told me that she hadn't been expecting anyone else—only you.'

Deborah gaped at him. 'She said that? But. . . .' But what, she thought frantically—perhaps what Trudi had said was true, perhaps she hadn't expected Claude. But on the other hand he had told her that he had come to fetch something and that Trudi was an old friend.

'Oh, please, do let me try and explain,' she begged, and met with a decided: 'No, Deborah—there is really no need.'

She stared at him wordlessly. No, she supposed, of course there was no need; his very indifference made that plain enough. It just didn't matter; she didn't matter either. She closed her eyes on the bitter thought, all the more bitter because she had thought, just once or twice lately, that she was beginning to matter just a little to him.

She opened her eyes again and went past him and down the stairs. Trudi was in the hall. Deborah gave her a look empty of all expression and opened the door on to the square. It looked peaceful and quiet under the late afternoon sky, but she didn't notice that; she didn't notice anything.

Once in the house, she raced up to her room and dragged out a case and started to stuff it with clothes. There was money in her purse, enough to get her to England—she couldn't go home, not just yet at any rate, not until she had sorted her thoughts out. She would go to Aunt Mary; her remote house by Hadrian's Wall was exactly the sort of place she wanted—a long, long way from Amsterdam, and Gerard.

She was on her way downstairs with her case when the front door opened and Gerard came in. He shut it carefully and stood with his back to it.

'I must talk to you, Deborah,' his voice was quiet and compelling. 'There's plenty of time if you're going for the night boat train. I'll drive you to the station—if you still want to go.'

Deborah swept across the hall, taking no notice, but at the door, of course, she was forced to stop; only then did she say: 'I'll get a taxi, thank you— perhaps you will let me pass.'

'No, I won't, my dear. You'll stay and hear what I have to say. Afterwards, if you still wish it, you shall go. But first I must explain.' He took the case from her and set it on the floor and then went back to lean against the door. 'Deborah, I have been very much at fault—I'm not sure what I thought when I saw Claude this afternoon. I only know that I was more angry than I have ever been before in my life, and my anger blinded me. After you had gone Trudi told me the truth—that Claude had come to see her. She is going to Nice with him, but they had planned it otherwise—I was to know nothing about it until I arrived in the morning and found a letter from her on my desk.' He smiled thinly. 'It seems that since Claude could not have my wife, he must make do with my secretary. None of this is an excuse for my treatment of you, Deborah, for which I am both ashamed and sorry. What would you like to do?'

'Go away,' said Deborah, her voice thick with tears she would rather have died than shed. 'I've an aunt—if I could go and stay with her, just for a little while, just to—to ... I've not been much of a success—I'd do better to go back to my old job.'

He said urgently: 'No, that's not true. No man could have had a more loyal and understanding wife. It is I who have failed you and I am only just beginning to see ... perhaps we could start again. You really want to go?' He paused and went on briskly: 'Come then, I'll take you to the station.'

If only he would say that he would miss her— She thought of a dozen excuses for staying and came up with the silliest. 'What about your dinner, and Wim—and Sien?'

'I'll see to everything,' he told her comfortably. 'You're sure that you have enough clothes with you?'

Deborah looked at him in despair; he was relieved that she was going. She nodded without speaking, having not the least idea what she had packed and not caring, and followed him out to the car. At the station he bought her ticket, stuffed some money into her handbag and saw her on to the train. She thought her heart would break as it slid silently away from the platform, leaving him standing there.

By the time she reached Aunt Mary's she was tired out and so unhappy that nothing mattered at all any more. She greeted her surprised relation with a story in which fact and fiction were so hopelessly jumbled together that they made no sense at all, and then burst into tears. She felt better after that and Aunt Mary being a sensible woman not given to asking silly questions, she was led to the small bedroom at the back of the little house, told to unpack, given a nourishing meal and ordered with mild authority to go to bed and sleep the clock round. Which she did, to wake to the firm conviction that she had been an utter fool to leave Gerard—perhaps he wouldn't want her back; he'd positively encouraged her to go, hadn't he? Could he be in love with some girl at long last and wish to put an end to their marriage and she not there to stop, if she were able, such nonsense? The idea so terrified her that she jumped out of bed and dressed at a great speed as though that would help in some way, but when she got downstairs and Aunt Mary took one look at her strained face, she said: 'You can't rush things, my dear, nor must you imagine things. Now all you need is patience, for although I'm not clear exactly what the matter is, you can be certain that it will all come right in the end if only you will give it time. Now go for a good long walk and come back with an appetite.'

Aunt Mary was right, of course. After three days of long walks, gentle talk over simple meals and the dreamless sleep her tiredness induced, Deborah began to feel better; she was still dreadfully unhappy, but at least she could be calm about it now. It would have been nice to have given way to tears whenever she thought about Gerard, which was every minute of the day, but that would not do, she could see that without Aunt Mary telling her so. In a day or two she would write a letter to him, asking him—she didn't know what she would ask him; perhaps inspiration would come when she picked up her pen.

The weather changed on the fourth day; layers of low cloud covered the moors, the heather lost its colour, the empty countryside looked almost frightening. There was next to no traffic on the road any more and even the few cottages which could be seen from Aunt Mary's windows had somehow merged themselves into the moorland around them so that they were almost invisible. But none of these things were reasons to miss her walk. She set off after their midday meal, with strict instructions to be back for tea and on no account to go off the road in case the mist should come down.

Sound advice which Deborah forgot momentarily when she saw an old ruined cottage some way from the road. It looked interesting, and without thinking, she tramped across the heather towards it. It was disappointing enough when she reached it, being nothing but an empty shell, but there was a dip beyond it with a small dewpond. She walked on to have a closer look and then wandered on, quite forgetful of her aunt's words. She had gone quite a distance when she saw the mist rolling towards her. She thought at first that it must be low-lying clouds which would sweep away, but it was mist, creeping forward at a great rate, sneaking up on her, thickening with every yard. She had the good sense to turn towards the road before it enveloped her entirely, but by then it was too late to see where she was going.

Shivering a little in its sudden chill, she sat down; probably it would lift very shortly. If she stayed where she was she would be quite safe. It would be easy to get back to the road as soon as she could see her way. It got too cold to sit after a time, so she got to her feet, stamping them and clapping her hands and trying to keep in one spot. And it was growing dark too; a little thread of fear ran through her head—supposing the mist lasted all night? It was lonely country—a few sheep, no houses within shouting distance, and the road she guessed to be a good mile away. She called herself a fool and stamped her feet some more.

It was quite dark and the mist was at its densest when she heard voices. At first she told herself that she was imagining things, but they became louder as they drew closer—children's voices, all talking at once.

'Hullo there!' she shouted, and was greeted by silence. 'Don't be frightened, I'm by myself and lost too. Shall we try and get together?'

This time there was a babble of sound from all around her. 'We're lost too.' The voice was on a level with her waist. 'Miss Smith went to get help, but it got dark and we started to walk. We're holding hands.'

'Who are you, and how many?' asked Deborah. Someone small brushed against her and a cold little hand found her arm. 'Oh, there you are,' it said tearfully. 'We're so glad to find someone—it's so dark. We're a school botany class from St Julian's, only Miss Smith lost the way and when the mist came she thought it would be quicker if she went for help. She told us to stay where we were, but she didn't come back and we got frightened.' The voice ended on a sob and Deborah caught the hand in her own and said hearteningly: 'Well, how lucky we've met—now we're together we've nothing to be afraid of. How many are there of you?'

'Eight—we're still holding hands.'

'How very sensible of you. May I hold hands too, then we can tell each other our names.'

There was a readjustment in the ranks of the little girls; the circle closed in on her. Deborah guessed that they were scared stiff and badly needed her company. 'Who's the eldest of you?' she enquired.

'Doreen—she's eleven.'

'Splendid!' What was so splendid about being eleven? she thought, stifling a giggle. 'I expect the mist will lift presently and we shall be able to walk to the road. It's not far.'

'It's miles,' said a plaintive voice so that Deborah went on cheerfully, 'Not really, and I can find it easily. My name's Deborah, by the way. How about stamping our feet to keep warm?'

They stamped until they were tired out. Deborah, getting a little desperate, suggested: 'Let's sit down. I know it's a bit damp, but if we keep very close to each other we shall keep warm enough. Let's sing.'

The singing was successful, if a little out of tune. They worked their way through 'This old man, he played one', the School Song, 'Rule Britannia' and a selection of the latest pop tunes. It was while they were getting their breath after these musical efforts that Deborah heard a shout. It was a nice, cheerful sound, a loud hullo in a man's voice, answered immediately by a ragged and very loud chorus of mixed screams and shouts from the little girls.

'Oh, that won't do at all,' said Deborah quickly. 'He'll get confused. We must all shout together at the same time. Everyone call "Here" when I've counted three.'

The voice answered them after a few moments, sometimes tantalizingly close, sometimes at a distance. After what seemed a long time, Deborah saw a faint glow ahead of them. A torch. 'Walk straight ahead,' she yelled, 'you're quite close.'

The glow got brighter, wavering from side to side and going far too slowly. 'Come on,' she shouted, 'you're almost here!'

The faint glow from the torch was deceptive in the mist, for the next thing she knew Gerard was saying from the gloom above her head, 'A fine healthy pair of lungs, dear girl—I've never been so glad to hear your voice, though I'm glad you don't always bellow like that.'

Surprise almost choked her. 'Gerard! Gerard, is it really you? How marvellous—how could you possibly know....'

'Your Aunt Mary told me that you had gone for a walk and it seemed a good idea to drive along the road to meet you. When the mist got too thick I parked the car, and then it was I heard these brats squealing,' there were muffled giggles to interrupt him here, 'and I collected them as I came.'

'You haven't got the botany class from St Julian's too?' she gasped. 'You can't have—I've got them here.'

'Indeed I have—or a part of it. A Miss Smith went for help and left them bunched together, but being the little horrors they are, they wandered off.'

'There aren't any missing?'

'No—we counted heads, as it were. Seven young ladies—very young ladies.'

Deborah had found his arm and was clutching it as though he might disappear at any moment. 'I've got eight of them here. What must we do, Gerard?'

'Why, my dear, stay here until the mist goes again. The car is up on the road, once we can reach it I can get you all back to Twice Brewed in no time at all.' He sounded so matter-of-fact about it that she didn't feel frightened any more. 'Your aunt has got everything organised by now, I imagine. She seemed to be a remarkably resourceful woman.' His hand sought and found hers and gave it a reassuring squeeze. 'In the meantime, I suggest that we all keep together, and don't let any of you young ladies dare to let go of hands. Supposing we sit?'

There was a good deal of giggling and a tremendous amount of shuffling and shoving and pushing before everyone was settled, sitting in a tight circle. Deborah, with Gerard's great bulk beside her, felt quite light-hearted, and the children, although there was a good deal of whining for something to eat, cheered up too, so that for a time at least, there was a buzz of talk, but gradually the shrill voices died down until there was silence and, incredibly, she dozed too, to wake shivering a little with the cold despite the arm around her shoulders. She whispered at once in a meek voice: 'I didn't mean to go to sleep, I'm sorry,' and felt the reassuring pressure of Gerard's hand.

'Not to worry. I think they have all nodded off, but we had better have a roll-call when they wake to be on the safe side.'

'Yes. I wonder what the time is, it's so very dark.'

'Look up,' he urged her, quietly. 'Above our heads.'

By some freak of nature the mist had parted itself, revealing a patch of inky sky, spangled with stars. 'Oh, lovely!' breathed Deborah. 'Only they don't seem real.'

'Of course they're real,' his whisper was bracing. 'It's the mist which isn't real. The stars have been there all the time, and always will be, only sometimes we don't see them—rather like life.' He sighed and she wondered what he meant. 'You see that bright one, the second star from the right?'

She said that yes, she could see it very well.

'That's our star,' he told her surprisingly, and when she repeated uncertainly 'Ours?' he went on: 'Do you not know that for every star in the heavens there is a man and a woman whose destinies are ruled by it? Perhaps they never meet, perhaps they meet too late or too soon, but just once in a while they meet at exactly the right moment and their destinies and their lives become one.'

In the awful, silent dark, anything would sound true; Deborah allowed herself a brief dream in which she indeed shared her destiny with Gerard, dispelled it by telling herself that the mist was making her fanciful, and whispered back: 'How do you know it's our star—it's ridiculous.'

'Of course it's ridiculous,' he agreed affably, and so readily that she actually felt tears of disappointment well into her eyes. 'But it's a thought that helps to pass the time, isn't it? Go to sleep again.'

And such was the calm confidence in his voice that she did as she was told, to waken in the bitter cold of the autumn dawn to an unhappy chorus of little girls wanting their mothers, their breakfasts, and to go home. Deborah was engulfed in them with no ears for anything else until she heard watery giggles coming from Gerard's other side, and his voice, loud and cheerful, declaring that they were all going to jump up and down and every few minutes bellow like mad. 'It's getting light; there will be people about soon.' He sounded quite positive about that. So they jumped and shouted, and although the mist was as thick as it ever was, at least they got warm, and surely any minute now the mist would roll away.

It did no such thing, however. They shouted

themselves hoarse, but there was no reply from the grey blanket around them. First one child and then another began to cry, and Deborah, desperately trying to instil a false cheer into her small unhappy companions, could hear Gerard doing the same, with considerably more success so that she found herself wondering where she had got the erroneous idea that he wasn't particularly keen on children. She remembered all at once what he had said about Sasja who hadn't wanted babies—the hurt must have gone deep. It seemed to her vital to talk about it even at so unsuitable a time and she was on the point of doing so when the mist folded itself up and disappeared. It was hard not to laugh; the little girls were still gathered in a tight circle, clutching each other's hands. They were white-faced and puffy-eyed, each dressed in the school uniform of St Julian's—grey topcoats and round grey hats with brims, anchored to their small heads by elastic under their chins. Some of them even had satchels over their shoulders and most of the hats were a little too large and highly unbecoming.

There was an excited shout as they all stood revealed once more and a tendency to break away until Gerard shouted to them to keep together still. 'A fine lot we would look,' he pointed out good-naturedly, 'if the mist comes back and we all get lost again.' He looked round at Deborah and smiled. 'We'll hold hands again, don't you think, and make for the road.'

They were half way there when they saw the search party—the local police, several farmers and the quite distraught Miss Smith who, when they met, burst into tears, while her botany class, with a complete lack of feeling for her distress and puffed up with a great sense of importance, told everyone severally and in chorus just how brave and resourceful they had been. It took a few minutes to sort them into the various cars and start the short journey to St Julian's.

Deborah found herself sitting beside Gerard, with four of the smallest children crammed in the back. She was weary and untidy, but when he suggested he should drop her off at Aunt Mary's as they went past, she refused.

On their way back from the school she began. 'How did...?' and was stopped by a quiet: 'Not now, dear girl, a hot bath and breakfast first.'

So it was only when they had breakfasted and she was sitting drowsily before a roaring fire in Aunt Mary's comfortable sitting room that she tried again. 'How did you know that I was here?'

'I telephoned your mother.'

'Oh—did she ask—that is, did she wonder....'

'If she did, she said nothing. Your mother is a wise woman, Deborah.'

'Why did you come?'

He was lying back, very much at his ease, in a high-backed chair, his eyes half shut. 'I felt I needed a break from work, it seemed a good idea to bring the car over and see if you were ready to come back.' He added: 'Smith is breaking his heart—think about it. Why not go to bed now, and get a few hours' sleep?'

Deborah got up silently. Smith might be breaking his doggy heart, but what about Gerard? There was no sign of even a crack; he was his usual calm, friendly self again, and no more. She went up to her little room and slept for hours, and when she came downstairs Aunt Mary was waiting for her.

'I told you to have patience, Debby,' she remarked with satisfaction. 'Everything will come right without you lifting a finger, mark my words.'

So when Gerard came in from the garden presently, she told him that she was ready to go back with him when he wished. She woke several times in the night and wondered, despite Aunt Mary's certainty, if she had made the right decision.

CHAPTER NINE

It was two days before they returned to Amsterdam, two days during which Gerard, who had become firm friends with Aunt Mary, dug the garden, chopped wood and did odd jobs around the house, as well as driving the two ladies into Carlisle to do some shopping.

They left after lunch, to catch the Hull ferry that evening, and Deborah, who had been alternately dreading and longing for an hour or so of Gerard's company, with the vague idea of offering to part with him and the even vaguer hope that he would tell her how much he had missed her, was forced to sit beside him in the car while he sustained a conversation about aunt Mary, the beauties of the moors, the charm of the small girls they had met and the excellence of his hostess's cooking. Each time Deborah tried to bring the conversation round to themselves he somehow baulked her efforts; in the end, she gave up, and when they reached Hull, what with getting the car on board, arranging to have dinner and their cabins, there wasn't much need to talk. Quite frustrated, she pleaded a headache directly they had finished dinner and retired to her cabin. She joined him for an early breakfast, though, because he had asked her to; he had, he told her, an appointment quite early in the morning at the hospital and didn't wish to waste any time.

He talked pleasantly as they took the road to Amsterdam and Deborah did her best to match his mood, but at the house he didn't come in with her, only unloaded her case and waited until Wim had opened the door before he drove away. She followed Wim inside. Gerard hadn't said when he would be home, nor had he spoken of themselves. She spent a restless day until he came home soon after tea and, as usual, went to his study. But before he could reach the door she was in the hall, a dozen things she wanted to say buzzing in her head. In the end she asked foolishly: 'What about Trudi? Did you get someone to take her place?'

He had halted and stood looking at her with raised eyebrows. 'Oh, yes—a middle-aged married woman, very sober and conscientious. You must go and see her for yourself some day.'

Deborah was left standing in the hall, her mouth open in surprise. Did he suppose her to be jealous of something absurd like that? She mooned back into the sitting room, Smith at her heels. Of course she was jealous; he filled her with rage, he was exasperating and indifferent, but she was still jealous. She would have to cure that, she told herself sternly, if she was to have any peace of mind in the future—the uncertain future, she had to allow, and wondered why Gerard had wanted her back. But if she had hoped to see a change in his manner towards her, she was doomed to disappointment. He was a quiet man by nature, he seemed to her to be even quieter now, and sometimes she caught him staring at her in a thoughtful manner; it was a pity that his habit of drooping the lids over his eyes prevented her from seeing their expression. There was no hint of a return of those few strange moments on the moor; they had been make-believe, she told herself, and took pains to take up the smooth, neat pattern of their life together as though it had never been ruffled out of its perfection.

She visited his family, arranged a dinner party for a medical colleague who was coming from Vienna and bought yet another new dress to wear at it. It was a very pretty dress, fine wool in soft greens and pinks, with a wide skirt. It would go very well with Tante Emmiline's garnets and perhaps, she hoped wistfully, Gerard might notice it. She hung it carefully in her clothes cupboard and went to get ready for the orphans' hour and for a number of muddled but sincere reasons, took almost every penny of her remaining allowance and when she reached the orphanage gate, stuffed the money into the alms box hung upon it, accompanying the action with a hotch-potch of wordless prayers—and later, when one of them was answered, took fresh heart. For Gerard noticed the new dress; indeed, he stood looking at her for so long that she became a little shy under his steady gaze and asked in a brittle little voice: 'Is there something wrong? Don't you like my dress?' She achieved a brittle laugh too. 'A pity, because it's too late to change it now.'

His eyes narrowed and a little smile just touched the corners of his mouth. 'Far too late, Deborah,' he said quietly, 'and I wouldn't change a single....' his voice altered subtly. 'The dress is delightful and you look charming.' He turned away as he spoke and the old-fashioned door bell tinkled through the house. 'Our guests, my dear. Shall we go and meet them?'

The other prayers must have become mislaid on the way, thought Deborah miserably as she got ready for bed later that evening, for when their guests had gone Gerard had told her that he would be going to Vienna for a five-day seminar in a day's time. When he had asked her if she would like him to bring back anything for her she had replied woodenly that no, there was nothing, thank you, and made some gratuitous remark about a few days of peace and quiet and now was her chance to take the new Fiat and go and see Abigail, who was still in Friesland.

Gerard had paused before he spoke. 'Why not?' he agreed affably, and looked up from the letters he was scanning. 'When is the baby due—several months, surely.'

'Almost six. I've knitted a few things, I'll take them with me.'

He nodded and went to open the door for her. 'Good idea.' He patted her kindly on the shoulder as she passed him. 'Sleep well, my dear,' and as an afterthought: 'I had no idea that you could knit.'

The pansy eyes smouldered. 'It's something I do while you're away or working in your study. I get through quite an amount.' Her voice was very even and she added a pleasant: 'Good night, Gerard.'

She didn't see him at breakfast, although he had left a scribbled note by her plate saying that he would be home for lunch—not later than one o'clock.

But it was later than that, it was six in the evening. She had eaten her lunch alone, telling herself that was what being a surgeon's wife meant; something she had known about and expected; it happened to all doctors' wives—the young houseman's bride, the G.P.'s lady, the consultant's wife, they all had to put up with it and so would she, only in their cases, a shared love made it easier. Deborah sighed, and loving him so much, hoped with all her heart that he, at least, was satisfied with their marriage. Apparently no more was to be said about Claude or any of the events connected with him, and in any case it was too late for recriminations now—besides, she wasn't sure if she had any; living with him, in the house he loved and which she had come to love too, was infinitely better than never seeing him again.

She was in the garden playing with Smith when he joined her. He looked weary and a little grim and she said at once: 'I've a drink ready for you—come inside,' and then because she couldn't bear to see him looking like that: 'Must you go tomorrow, Gerard? Is it important?'

He took the glass from her and smiled in a way which somehow disturbed her. 'Yes, Deborah, I think it's very important—I have to be sure of something, you see. It involves someone else besides myself.'

An icy finger touched her heart and she turned away from him. 'Oh, well, I'll telephone Abigail.'

'I thought you had already arranged to visit her.'

'No—it had quite slipped my mind,' she improvised hastily, because the reason she hadn't telephoned was because she had hoped, right until this last moment, that he might suggest her going with him, but he wouldn't do that now. Hadn't he said that there was someone else? She wondered if he had meant a patient and very much doubted it. She telephoned Abigail there and then, being very gay about it.

She wished Gerard a cheerful goodbye after breakfast the next morning and after a fine storm of weeping in her room afterwards, dressed herself and drove the car to Friesland where she received a delighted welcome from Abigail and Dominic. They had come out to meet her, walking together, not touching, but so wrapped together in happiness so secure and deep that she could almost see it. For a moment she wished she hadn't come, but later, laughing and talking in their comfortable sitting room, it wasn't so bad. Indeed the day went too quickly. Driving back Deborah contemplated the four days left before Gerard should come back. There was, of course, the orphans' hour, but that wasn't until Thursday. She would have to fill the days somehow. She spent the rest of the journey devising a series of jobs which would keep her occupied for the next day or two.

She was a little early when she got to the orphanage on Thursday evening, but although it still wanted five minutes to the hour, the children were already assembled in the long, bare room, At least, thought Deborah, as she took off her coat and prepared for the next hour's boisterous games, the evening would pass quickly, and the next day Gerard would be back. She longed to see him, just as she dreaded his return, wondering what he would have to tell her, or perhaps he would have nothing to say, and that would be even harder to bear.

She turned to the task in hand, greeting the children by name as they milled around her, separat-

ing the more belligerent bent on the inevitable
fight, picking up and soothing those who, just as
inevitably, had fallen down and were now howling
their eyes out. Within five minutes, however, she
had a rousing game of 'Hunt the Slipper' going—a
hot favourite with the orphans because it allowed a
good deal of legitimate screaming and running
about. This was followed by 'Twos and Threes'. A
good deal of discreet cheating went on here; the
very small ones, bent on getting there first, were
prone to fall on their stomachs and bawl until
Deborah raced to pick them up and carry them in
triumph to the coveted place in the circle.

There was a pause next, during which she did
her best to tidy her hair which had escaped most of
its pins and hung most untidily around her shoulders. But it took too long, besides, there was no one
to see—the children didn't care and she certainly
didn't. 'Grandmother's Steps' was to be the final
game of the evening, and Deborah, her face to the
wall, listened to the stampede of what the orphans
imagined were their creeping little feet and
thanked heaven that there was no one below them
or close by. She looked over her shoulder, pretending not to see the hasty scramble of the slower children to achieve immobility, and turned to the wall
again. Once more, she decided, and then she would
declare them all out and bring the game to a satis-
factory conclusion.

She counted ten silently and turned round. 'All
of you,' she began in her fragmental Dutch which
the children understood so well. 'You're out ... I
saw you move....' Her voice died in her throat and
her breath left her; behind the children, half way
down the room, stood Gerard.

He came towards her slowly, pausing to pat a small tow-coloured head of hair or lift the more persistent hangers-on out of his way. When he reached her he said with a kind of desperate quietness: 'I thought I should never find you—such a conspiracy of silence....'

Her hand went to cover her open mouth. 'Wim and Marijke, they knew—they discovered. They were sweet about it—don't be angry with them.' She searched his calm face for some sign; his eyes were hooded, there was the faintest smile on his mouth; she had no idea what his true feelings were. She went on earnestly: 'You see, it's a Catholic convent and you—your family are Calvinists.' Her look besought him to understand. 'You—you don't mix very well, do you? Separate schools and hospitals and....'

'Orphanages?' he offered blandly.

She nodded wordlessly and lapsed into thought, to say presently:

'Besides, you're home a day early.'

'Ah,' the lids flew open revealing blue eyes whose gleam made her blink. 'Am I to take it that that is a disappointment to you?'

'Disappointment?' Her voice rose alarmingly. There were small hands tugging at her skirt, hoarse little voices chanting an endless 'Debby' at her, but she hardly noticed them; she had reached the end of her emotional tether.

'Disappointment? Disappointment? This week's been endless—they always are when you go away. I'm sick and tired—I won't go on like this, being a kind of genteel housekeeper and wondering all the time—every minute of every day—where you are and what you're doing and pretending that I don't care. . . .'

She was in full spate, but the rest of it never got said; she was gripped in an embrace which bade fair to crack her ribs, and kissed with a fierceness to put an end to all her doubts.

'How can a man be so blind?' Gerard spoke into her ear and the children's voices faded quite away from her senses. 'The star was there, only I didn't want to see it. I wanted to stay in the mist I had made—the nice safe mist which wouldn't allow anything to interfere with my work, because that was all I thought I had left. And yet I suppose I knew all the time. . . .' He loosed his hold for the fraction of a minute and looked down into her face. 'I love you, my darling girl,' he said, and kissed her again; a pleasant state of affairs which might have gone on for some time if it hadn't been for the insistent pushes, tugs and yells from the orphans—it was story time and they knew their rights.

It was Deborah who broke the spell between them. 'My darling, I have to tell them a story—just until seven o'clock.' She smiled at him, her pansy eyes soft with love; he kissed her once more, a gentle kiss this time, and let her go. 'A fairy story,' she told him. ' "Rose Red and Rose White" . . .'

His mouth twitched into a faint smile. 'In which language, dear heart?' he asked.

'Both, of course—I don't know half the words.' She smiled again. 'Heaven knows what they're thinking of us at this moment!'

'Nor I, though I'm very sure of what I'm thinking about you, but that can wait.'

He pulled up the tattered old music stool so that she could sit on it and the children jostled happily against each other, getting as close as they could.

186

'Rose Red and Rose White,' began Deborah in a voice lilting with not quite realized happiness, and the children fell silent as she plunged into the story, using a wild mixture of Dutch and English words and a wealth of gestures and mime and never doubting that the children understood every word, which, strangely enough, they did. They sat enrapt, their small mouths open, not fidgeting, and two of them had climbed on to Gerard's knees where he sat on one of the low window seats, listening to his wife's clear voice mangling the Dutch language. She had reached a dramatic point in her narrative when the room shook and trembled under the tones of the great bell from the church across the road.

'Seven o'clock,' said Deborah, very conscious of Gerard's look. 'We'll finish next week,' and added, 'Sweeties!' at the top of her voice, producing at the same time the bag of toffees which signalled the end of play hour.

She was marshalling her small companions into a more or less tidy line when the faint dry tinkle of the front door bell whispered its way along the passage and up the stairs. It was followed almost at once by the Mother Superior, who greeted Deborah warmly, the children with an all-embracing smile, and an extended hand for Gerard, admirably concealing any surprise she might have felt at finding him there.

'The little ones have been good?' she asked Deborah.

'They always are, Mother. Do you want me to come on Friday next week, or is it to be Thursday again?'

The nice elderly face broke into a smile. 'You

will have the time?' The pale blue eyes studied Gerard, the hint of a question in their depths.

'I approve of anything my wife does,' he told her at once, 'even though you and I are in—er—opposite camps.'

She answered him gravely, although her eyes were twinkling. 'That is nice to know, Mijnheer van Doorninck. You like children?'

He was looking at Deborah. 'Yes, Mother, although I'm afraid I've not had much to do with them.'

'That will arrange itself,' the old lady assured him, 'when you have children of your own.' She glanced at Deborah, smiling faintly. 'Thank you for your kind help, my child. And now we must go.'

The line of orphans stirred its untidy ranks; they hadn't understood anything of what had been said, and they wanted their supper, but first of all they wanted to be kissed goodnight by Debby, who always did. A small sigh went through the children as she started at the top of the line, bending over each child and hugging it, until, the last one kissed, they clattered out of the room and down the stairs. Deborah stood in the middle of the room, listening to the sound of their feet getting fainter and fainter until she could hear it no longer. Only then did she turn round.

Gerard was still by the window. He smiled and opened his arms wide and she ran to him, to be swallowed up most comfortably in their gentle embrace.

'My adorable little wife,' he said, and his words were heaven in her ears; she was five foot ten in her stockings and no slim wand of a girl; no one had ever called her little before. Perhaps Gerard, from his vantage point of another four inches, really did find her small. She lifted a glowing face for his face, and presently asked:

'You're not angry about the orphans?'

'No, my love. Indeed, they are splendid practice for you.'

She leaned back in his arms so that she could see his face. 'You're not going to start an orphanage?'

'Hardly that, dear heart—I hope that our children will always have a home.'

'Oh.' She added idiotically: 'There are twenty-eight of them.'

He kissed the top of her head. 'Yes? It seemed like ten times that number. Even so, I would hardly expect ...!' She felt his great chest shake with silent laughter. 'A fraction of that number would do very nicely, don't you agree?' And before she could answer: 'Don't you want to know why I have come back early?'

'Yes—though it's enough that you're here.' She leaned up to kiss him.

'Simple. I found myself unable to stay away from you a moment longer. At first, I wanted to keep everything cool and friendly and impersonal between us, and then, over the weeks, I found it harder and harder to leave you, even to let you out of my sight, and yet I wouldn't admit that I loved you, although I knew in my heart—I could have killed Claude.'

'But you let me go away—all the way to Aunt Mary's....'

'My darling, I thought that I had destroyed any chance of making you love me.'

'But I did love you—I've loved you for years....'

189

He held her very close. 'You gave no sign, Debby —but all the same I had to follow you, and then I found you in the mist with all those little girls in their strange round hats.'

Deborah laughed into his shoulder. 'You showed me our star,' she reminded him.

'It's still there,' he told her. 'We're going to share it for the rest of our lives.'

He turned her round to face the window. 'There —you see?'

The sky was dark, but not as dark as the variegated roofs pointing their gables into it, pointing, all of them, to the stars. The carillon close by played its little tune for the half hour and was echoed a dozen times from various parts of Amsterdam. It was all peaceful and beautiful, but Deborah was no longer looking at it. She had turned in her husband's arms to face him again, studying his face.

'Are we going home?' she asked, when he had kissed her just once more, she said, 'Our home, darling Gerard.'

'Our home, my love, although for me, home will always be where you are.'

There was only one answer to that. She wreathed her arms round his neck and kissed him.

Golden Harlequin Library

A Treasury of Harlequin Romances!

Many of the all time favorite Harlequin Romance Novels have not been available, until now, since the original printing. But on this special introductory offer, they are yours in an exquisitely bound, rich gold hardcover with royal blue imprint. Three complete unabridged novels in each volume. And the cost is so very low you'll be amazed!

Handsome, Hardcover Library Editions at Paperback Prices! ONLY $1.95 each volume. or $11.70 the set

This very special collection of classic Harlequin Romances would be a distinctive addition to your library. And imagine what a delightful gift they'd make for any Harlequin reader!

Volumes 43 to 48 Just Published!
See following page.

x

GOLDEN
HARLEQUIN LIBRARY

$11.70
per set

Each volume contains 3 complete
Harlequin Romances

$1.95
each volume

To: Harlequin Reader Service, Dept. G 403
M.P.O. Box 707, Niagara Falls, N.Y. 14302
Canadian address: Stratford, Ont., Canada

☐ Please send me complete listing of the 48 Golden Harlequin Library Volumes.

☐ Please send me the Golden Harlequin Library editions I have indicated above.

I enclose $_____ (No C.O.D.'s) To help defray postage and handling costs, please add 50c.

Name _____

Address _____

City/Town _____

State/Province _____ Zip_____

G 403